CHINESE POETRY

THROUGH

THE WORDS OF

THE PEOPLE

CHINESE POETRY

中國詩

THROUGH

THE WORDS OF

THE PEOPLE

EDITED BY

BONNIE

McCANDLESS

BALLANTINE BOOKS
NEW YORK

Sale of this book without a front cover may be unauthorized. If this book is coverless, it may have been reported to the publisher as "unsold or destroyed" and neither the author nor the publisher may have received payment for it.

An Available Press Book
Published by Ballantine Books
Copyright © 1991 by Bonnie McCandless

All rights reserved under International and Pan-American Copyright Conventions. Published in the United States by Ballantine Books, a division of Random House, Inc., New York, and simultaneously in Canada by Random House of Canada Limited, Toronto.

Owing to space limitations, permissions to reprint previously published material appear on page 128.

Library of Congress Catalog Card Number: 90-93520

ISBN: 0-345-37135-6

Cover design by Don Munson

Cover calligraphy by Yasuko Shimizu

Text design by Holly Johnson

Manufactured in the United States of America

First Edition: October 1991

10 9 8 7 6 5 4 3 2 1

*Dedicated, with love,
to the memory of my mother,
Lucie B. McCandless*

CONTENTS

INTRODUCTION		ix
ONE	Ancient Chinese Poetry	3
TWO	Ch'ü Yüan: China's First Great Poet	15
THREE	Poetry of the Recluse	23
FOUR	Famous T'ang Dynasty Poets	33
FIVE	Chinese Women and Poetry	49
SIX	Poetry in Music, Art, and Theatre	65
SEVEN	Modern Views and Voices	81
EIGHT	Poetry of Revolution	99
NINE	A New Poetry Emerges	113

INTRODUCTION

Chinese Poetry: Through the Words of the People is a collection of English translations of poems written in the Chinese language by the people of China—from the first poems recorded twenty-five hundred years ago to poems composed in 1989; from the feudal states of ancient China to the divided nations of the People's Republic of China and Nationalist China in Taiwan; from love songs and word games to impassioned expletives about war and revolution.

    The beauty of the imagery and the simplicity of the sentiment expressed in the poetry of China intrigues me. The Chinese language, however, is a different world entirely. Written as a pictograph, the Chinese character is a fascinating form of communication that developed over a span of three thousand years and is still being modified for contemporary literacy needs. I love Chinese calligraphy and have put brush to paper for the artistic pleasure of it, but I have no knowledge of the Chinese language. The richness of this collection, in fact, derives from a thrice-removed position: I am a student of translations by English and American scholars, who are themselves students of the Chinese language and literary forms, and the poet himself or herself is a student of Chinese life and landscape. Nuances and variations in meaning different from the original poet's experiences, interpreted by the reader's unique perspective, are what give poetry a timeless quality. My objective from the start was to bring together a sampler of the breadth and scope of Chinese poetry, and to illustrate how a literary tradition tells the story of the history and culture of a people. This is the essence of the subtitle "Through the Words of the People."

To the Chinese people the poetic form is a more natural form of expression than we Americans are accustomed to, and they have used it perhaps more spontaneously. Confucius wrote down over three thousand folk songs for the first collection of poetry from the people, and in the 1950s, as a result of a government-initiated campaign, over seven hundred volumes, containing a small fraction of the total number of verses written, were collected by national publishers. The Chinese write poems to each other instead of letters. They write poems to express mourning over the death of a beloved leader; hundreds were presented in Tiananmen Square after Zhou Enlai died.

In choosing this title, however, I do not mean to imply that all Chinese people write or read poetry; in fact, the great masses of Chinese peasantry have traditionally been excluded from education and are only now becoming literate. It is estimated that the largest readership for literature in China today is urban youth, and that they represent only ten percent of the population. The semieducated populace from the outer provinces read spy novels, mysteries, and romances, if they read at all. With that in mind, *the people* are neither speaking nor listening! And this is a familiar pattern among American readers. But Chinese poets have always spoken for the people and about them in a way that projects a sense of shared destiny and joint ownership of the poetic tradition.

How did I make my selections? I chose poems that represented an era, a style, a theme, a perspective, a mood, or a feeling. I wanted a variety and depth of subject matter. From among the many fine anthologies that have been published in this century I chose translations that had a poetic quality in English that I hoped matched the poetry of the original Chinese version. Translators have their own styles and I tried to avoid those whose renditions were more Western than Eastern, more wordy than imagistic. I did keep the translators' spellings, punctuations, and words precisely; so there may appear to be an inconsistency in editorial style among the poems. But I felt it was vital to preserve the translator's "poetic license" as well as the poet's.

I also used the old spellings—Li Po instead of Li Bai, Mao Tse-tung instead of Mao Zedong—only because most of the translations are in that tradition, and I had come to know the poets' names as old friends. Whenever possible I dated the poems to the year of composition, or the century, when that made more sense. I selected from the best-known poets according to critical acclaim and my own personal preference. Hundreds of volumes of English translations exist; it was not possible to be fair and include them all. Fortunately, there are many anthologies for further reading if this sampling sparks a specific interest in a poet or time or topic.

And that is my fervent hope—that in addition to broadening our international cultural awareness, this collection will make more accessible to wider American audiences the wisdom and beauty of these personal expressions. We Americans often grab what is closest, hear what is loudest, and enjoy our leisure moments in fragmented bits of time and space. Once we leave school, life becomes our best teacher and we lose the habit of reading to stimulate the brain or nourish the soul. Our entertainment becomes passive at best; we become lazy. Reading Chinese poetry can help restore an active participation in the world of ideas; indeed, poetry is particularly good for that because it comes in small doses, well-suited to our active life-styles. Keeping a book of poetry by your bedside can be a daily source of inspiration.

I do not write poetry, but I have found reading poetry to be a wonderful elixir when my spirits are worn or trampled. I always read a poem several times over, speaking it aloud when I can, and if I am able to let my imagination wander, I become, for an instant, that poet. I imagine I can see life through the poet's eyes, and I cry or laugh or shout as he or she does; I feel and think from a different place than my own. When I read Chinese poetry I am magically transported across the oceans to a land and way of life that are exotic yet natural and uncomplicated: I see delicate flowers and bamboo branches, black-haired people with shy smiles riding bicycles or dancing in slow-motion tai ch'i; I see a river with a single yellow sail winding its way to the horizon, a craggy mountain covered with majestic pine trees; I see red flags and a sea of green uniforms. As in this poem by a modern Chinese master poet, the images reveal a world and I enter:

MIDNIGHT

HSÜ CHIH-MO, 1925

At midnight, in a corner down the street
The shafts of lamplight were as dim as dreams.

The trees were drowned in mist.
No wonder people lost their way.

"You've wronged me, cruel enemy!"
She wept:—came no reply.

The dawn wind shook the tree-tops:
The fine flushed leaves of autumn fluttered down.
    (Translated by Harold Acton and Ch'en-hsiang)

I feel the poet's anguish, asking the question and finding no answer, but morning comes and autumn leaves fall; life continues. And the Chinese people will continue to speak to me through their poetry. I listen and I am moved.

CHINESE POETRY

THROUGH
THE WORDS OF
THE PEOPLE

ONE

ANCIENT CHINESE POETRY

The first collection of Chinese poetry came from the common people of the northern provinces during the Chou dynasty (1000–221 B.C.) and was known as the *Shih Ching*, or *Book of Songs*. Although the Chinese had been composing poems orally for centuries before this time, after a system of writing was invented, the poems were written down. Emperors hereafter made it a policy to collect the poems, or songs, for government agencies called "music bureaus." Similar to our oral folk tradition—workers chanting in the fields, young women preparing for their weddings, songs being sung for games, dances, and feasts—the songs find their best expression when recited aloud. Confucius used the folk poetry in his teachings, believing that they contained great wisdom, perhaps even the mystery of life itself. According to historians, it is he who selected 305 of the most popular songs for this collection around 600 B.C.

The poems celebrate the simple joys and sorrows of a people living close to nature. They are vignettes of emotions with the stories often masked or forgotten, full of colors, rituals, and seasons. They abound with nature symbolism and metaphors, repetitions of words and refrains. Many are sad and nostalgic, lamenting death and separation, expressing battle weariness, and protesting social injustices. The feudal system created slaves of peasants, men who went off to fight the warlord's battles and did not return. Women and children were left to tend the crops by themselves and their lonely cries of unhappiness filled the fields. The messages in the *Book of Songs* are direct and poignant, sensitive expressions of a people who already felt part of an ancient tradition: the oldest continuous poetic tradition in the world.

But the peasants told only one part of the story. Poets were composing ballads and writing verses filled with allusions to rulers, places, events, and legends—so tied to ancient China, in fact, that their meanings are often completely obscured. Scholars, statesmen, and other officials tried their hands at writing poetry, as purely political exercises. As entertainment for the emperors, court poets created clever wordplays and highly stylized tales which they recited to the ruling gentry. They were often full of sarcasm and wit, fanciful stories with moralistic endings. Even though Chinese society has always been intensely polarized—gold finery and the extravagance of the rulers next to the painful poverty of the peasants—poetry was an accepted and accessible form of expression for all the people.

During the Han Dynasty (206 B.C. to A.D. 221) another type of poetry became popular. These poems were often introduced by prose pieces and were longer, descriptive verses using meter and rhyme. Many were in the form of a debate and were thought to have as a primary purpose the instruction or reprimand of the emperor; some scholars believe the folk songs were collected for that purpose as well.

Selections here from the *Book of Songs* reflect the life of the common people. "The Wind" is an example of a rhyme-prose poem by Sung Yü, one of the best-known court poets of the third century B.C.

THE WIND

SUNG YÜ, 3RD CENTURY B.C.

King Hsiang of Ch'u was taking his ease in the Palace of the Orchid Terrace, with his courtiers Sung Yü and Chiang Ch'a attending him, when a sudden gust of wind came sweeping in. The king, opening wide the collar of his robe and facing into it, said, "How delightful this wind is! And I and the common people may share it together, may we not?"

But Sung Yü replied, "This wind is for Your Majesty alone. How could the common people have a share in it?"

"The wind," said the king, "is the breath of heaven and earth. Into every corner it unfolds and reaches; without choosing between high or low, exalted or humble, it touches everywhere. What do you mean when you say that this wind is for me alone?"

Sung Yü replied, "I have heard my teacher say that the twisted branches of the lemon tree invite the birds to nest, and hollows and cracks summon the wind. But the breath of the wind differs with the place which it seeks out."

"Tell me," said the king, "where does the wind come from?"

Sung Yü answered:

> "The wind is born from the land
> And springs up in the tips of the green duckweed.
> It insinuates itself into the valleys
> And rages in the canyon mouth,
> Skirts the corners of Mount T'ai
> And dances beneath the pines and cedars.
> Swiftly it flies, whistling and wailing;
> Fiercely it sputters its anger.

It crashes with a voice like thunder,
Whirls and tumbles in confusion,
Shaking rocks, striking trees,
Blasting the tangled forest.
Then, when its force is almost spent,
It wavers and disperses,
Thrusting into crevices and rattling door latches.
Clean and clear,
It scatters and rolls away.
Thus it is that this cool, fresh hero wind,
Leaping and bounding up and down,
Climbs over the high wall
And enters deep into palace halls.
With a puff of breath it shakes the leaves and flowers,
Wanders among the cassia and pepper trees,
Or soars over the swift waters.
It buffets the mallow flower,
Sweeps the angelica, touches the spikenard,
Glides over the sweet lichens and lights on willow shoots,
Rambling over the hills
And their scattered host of fragrant flowers.
After this, it wanders into the courtyard,
Ascends the jade hall in the north,
Clambers over gauze curtains,
Passes through the inner apartments,
And so becomes Your Majesty's wind.
When this wind blows on a man,
At once he feels a chill run through him,
And he sighs at its cool freshness.
Clear and gentle,
It cures sickness, dispels drunkenness,
Sharpens the eyes and ears,

Relaxes the body and brings benefit to men.
This is what is called the hero wind of Your Majesty."

"How well you have described it!" exclaimed the king. "But now may I hear about the wind of the common people?"

And Sung Yü replied:

"The wind of the common people
Comes whirling from the lanes and alleys,
Poking in the rubbish, stirring up the dust,
Fretting and worrying its way along.
It creeps into holes and knocks on doors,
Scatters sand, blows ashes about,
Muddles in dirt and tosses up bits of filth.
It sidles through hovel windows
And slips into cottage rooms.
When this wind blows on a man,
At once he feels confused and downcast.
Pounded by heat, smothered in dampness,
His heart grows sick and heavy,
And he falls ill and breaks out in a fever.
Where it brushes his lips, sores appear;
It strikes his eyes with blindness.
He stammers and cries out,
Not knowing if he is dead or alive.
This is what is called the lowly wind of the common people."

(Translated by Burton Watson)

SELECTIONS FROM THE *BOOK OF SONGS*
CIRCA 600 B.C.

EAST GATE WILLOWS

Willows outside the east gate
are thick with leaves; in the evening
she said she would meet me there,
I waited for her till dawn.
    Willows outside the east gate
    with leaves that would hide us well;
    she promised to be there,
    but I waited and watched till came
    the morning star.

(Translated by Rewi Alley)

THE ROEBUCK

In the wilds there lies a dead roebuck
Covered over with white rushes;
A girl is longing for love,
A fine fellow tempts her.

In the woods are bushes,
And in the wilds a dead deer
Bound with white rushes.
The girl is fair as jade.

"Oh, soft now and gently;
Don't touch my sash!
Take care, or the dog will bark!"

*(Translated by Yang Xianyi,
Gladys Yang, and Hu Shiguang)*

RABBIT GOES SOFT-FOOT

Rabbit goes soft-foot, pheasant's caught,
I began life with too much elan,
Troubles come to a bustling man.
    "Down Oh, and give me a bed!"
Rabbit soft-foot, pheasant's in trap,
I began life with a flip and flap,
Then a thousand troubles fell on my head,
    "If I could only sleep like the dead!"

Rabbit goes soft-foot, pheasant gets caught.
A youngster was always rushin' round,
Troubles crush me to the ground.
    I wish I could sleep and not hear a sound.

(Translated by Ezra Pound)

TALL STANDS THAT PEAR-TREE

Tall stands that pear-tree;
Its leaves are fresh and fair.
But alone I walk, in utter solitude.
True indeed, there are other men;
But they are not like children of one's own father.
Heigh, you that walk upon the road,
Why do you not join me?
A man that has no brothers,
Why do you not help him?

Tall stands that pear-tree;
Its leaves grow very thick.
Alone I walk and unbefriended.
True indeed, there are other men;
But they are not like the people of one's own clan.
Heigh, you that walk upon the road,
Why do you not join me?
A man that has no brothers,
Why do you not help him?

(Translated by Arthur Waley)

GRAIN FOR EMPEROR HUAN

The wheat is up, the barley
ripens; who goes to reap it then?
Only girls and old women;
the men are all conscripted
to fight the tribesmen; so came
small officials demanding horses,
big officials shouting for carts;
I speak for all the little people
who hardly dare give voice
to their thoughts.

(Translated by Rewi Alley)

CHINESE POETRY

KING WEN'S PARK DIVINE

When he planned to begin a spirit tower
folk rushed to the work-camp and overran
all the leisure of King Wen's plan;
old and young with never a call
had it up in no time at all.

The king stood in his "Park Divine,"
deer and doe lay there so fine,
so fine so sleek; birds of the air
flashed a white wing while fishes splashed
on wing-like fin in the haunted pool.

Great drums and gongs
hung on spiked frames
sounding to perfect rule and rote
about the king's calm crescent moat,
Tone unto tone, of drum and gong.

About the king's calm crescent moat
the blind musicians beat lizard skin
as the tune weaves out and in.

(Translated by Ezra Pound)

LAMENTATIONS #276

BIG rat, big rat,
Do not gobble our millet!
Three years we have slaved for you,
Yet you take no notice of us.
At last we are going to leave you
And go to that happy land;
Happy land, happy land,
Where we shall have our place.

BIG rat, big rat,
Do not gobble our corn!
Three years we have slaved for you,
Yet you give us no credit.
At last we are going to leave you
And go to that happy kingdom;
Happy kingdom, happy kingdom,
Where we shall get our due.

BIG rat, big rat,
Do not eat our rice-shoots!
Three years we have slaved for you,
Yet you did nothing to reward us.
At last we are going to leave you
And go to those happy borders;
Happy borders, happy borders
Where no sad songs are sung.

(Translated by Arthur Waley)

TWO

CH'Ü YÜAN: CHINA'S FIRST GREAT POET

The second collection of Chinese poems is attributed to the works of a single poet, Ch'ü Yüan (329–229 B.C.), from the state of Ch'u, south of the Yangtze River. Called *Ch'u Tz'u (Songs of the South)*, it was compiled around 300 B.C. The poet, Ch'ü Yüan, claimed royal ancestry and served as a loyal high minister to King Huai of Ch'u. Due to a personal or political difference—some say he opposed his lord's war policies; some say it was a case of slander by political rivals—he became estranged from his lord and was finally banished. Ch'ü Yüan roamed the countryside, particularly drawn to wild riverbanks, bewailing his fate. This collection contains the longest narrative poem to be recorded at that time, a 374-line lament called "Li Sao" or "Encountering Sorrow." Caught between the politics of man and the purity of the imagination, a place of desolation for the true poet's soul, Ch'ü Yüan's poetry has an intense, haunting quality.

Ch'u Tz'u also includes "Nine Songs," which, if not written by Ch'ü Yüan himself, were apparently collected and adapted by him as he traveled among the people. They appear to be based on shamanistic rituals that were performed with pantomime at court. They depict worshipers dressed in beautiful costumes, draped in fragrant flowers, conversing with deities. The meter is similar to the *Book of Songs*, but the imagery is mythical, often erotic. The speaker in the poems changes, but the mood remains one of ecstatic longing.

"Li Sao" represents a new poetic genre. It is longer, with powerful rhythm, eloquent imagery, and a single purpose. The poet recounts his noble ancestry and then sets off in a dragon-drawn chariot. He journeys to the gravesite of the sage Shun, where he vows not to compromise his virtue. He flies around searching unsuccessfully for a mate, complaining about the wicked state of affairs of the world, and referring to plants as allegorical political figures. Finally the poet travels to the K'un-lung Mountains in the west, where he tries to ascend to heaven but his horses refuse to advance, and the poem ends in despair.

On the fifth day of the fifth moon Ch'ü Yüan drowned himself in the Milo River. His suicide is celebrated every year with dragon festivals and rice offerings thrown on the water. Because of his beautiful poetry and the poignancy of his tragic end, Ch'ü Yüan is considered among the greatest of all Chinese poets.

CHINESE POETRY

SELECTIONS FROM *NINE SONGS*

THE LORD AMONG THE CLOUDS

I bathe in orchid water,
    wash my hair with scents,
put on colored robes,
    flower-figured.
The spirit, twisting and turning,
    poised now above,
radiant and shining
    in endless glory,
comes to take his ease
    in the Temple of Long Life,
and with the sun and moon
    to pair his brilliance.
Riding his dragon chariot,
    drawn like a god,
he hovers and soars,
    roaming the vastness;
spirit majestic,
    but now descended,
swiftly rising
    far off to the clouds.
He looks down on Chi-chou,
    the regions beyond,
crosses to the four seas;
    what land does he not visit?
I think of you, Lord,
    sighing,
You afflict my heart
    sorely, sorely!

(Translated by Burton Watson)

THE SPIRIT OF THE MOUNTAIN

It seemed as though
the spirit of the mountain
showed herself, clothed
in leaves and flowers, eyes
sparkling with beauty, lips
parted in laughter, as though
inviting one into loveliness;

> with the wild animals of the forest
> as steeds, and as guardsmen;
> precious woods to carve into chariots,
> flowers for standards, robes and
> girdles; so may the mountain spirit
> wander among the blossoms;

plucking them for her lover;
as for me,
under the dark bamboos,
their leaves keeping out the light,
alone do I stagger upward
over dangerous and difficult
paths;

> until by myself
> on the top of the mountain;
> looking below me at the clouds,
> sombre with the aftermath of sunset;
> gloom descends; an east wind rises,
> rain starts to fall;

the mountain spirit is secure
in her home; only I
am homeless, older
with each passing year;

never more to see
youth again;

> searching for herbs,
> I tear my way
> through tangled creepers
> over jagged stones; hating
> my enemies, with no hope
> to return to my home again;
> yet, even should there be one
> who thinks of me,
> how could he call me now?

After all,
I reflect
here in this mountain,
with the scent
of trees, springs to drink from,
shade beneath the pines
and cedars; maybe someone
still thinks of me,
yet fears to commit himself
in calling me;

> thunder crashes
> and the rain swishes down
> all the night through; wild
> beasts howl, and the storm
> tears through the trees
> making branches creak;
> I think of him and feel
> the futility of mere sorrow.

(Translated by Rewi Alley)

SELECTIONS FROM *LI SAO*

CH'Ü YÜAN

I am a descendant of Emperor Kao-yang;
My father's name was Po-yung.
When the constellation *She-t'i* pointed to the first month of
    the year,
On the day *keng-yin* I was born.
My father, observing the aspect of my birth,
Divined and chose for me auspicious names.
The personal name he gave me was Upright Model;
The formal name he gave me was Divine Balance.
. . . .

I hurried on, as though I could never catch up,
Afraid that the years would leave me behind.
In the morning I plucked mountain magnolias;
At evening I gathered sedges on the islets.
Days and months sped by, never stopping;
Springs and autumns gave way to each other.
I thought how the flowers were falling, the trees growing
    bare,
And feared my Fair One too would grow old.
Hold fast to youth and cast away the foul!
Why will you not change your ways?
Mount brave steeds and gallop forth!
Come, I will go before and show you the way.
. . . .

I ordered my phoenixes to fly aloft
And continue onward day and night.
Whirlwinds gathered together to meet me;
Leading clouds and rainbows, they came in greeting,
Joining and parting in wild confusion,

Rising and falling in jumbled array.
I commanded Heaven's porter to open for me,
But he leaned on the gate and eyed me with scorn.
. . . .

I thought that orchid could be trusted,
But he is faithless and a braggart.
He turns from beauty to follow the vulgar,
Yet expects to be ranked among the fragrant flowers.
. . . .

I curbed my will and slackened my pace,
My spirit soaring high in the distant regions.
I played the Nine Songs and danced the Shao music,
Stealing a little time for pleasure.
But as I ascended the brightness of heaven,
Suddenly I looked down and saw my old home,
My groom was filled with sadness, and the horses in their longing
Pulled about in the reins and refused to go on.
. . . .

It is over! There is no one in the kingdom who knows me!
Why long for my old city?
Since there is no one worthy to join me in just rule,
I will go to P'eng Hsien* in the place where he dwells.

(Translated by Burton Watson)

---

*Reputed to be a worthy minister of the Shang dynasty who, when his advice was unheeded, drowned himself in a river.

THREE

POETRY OF THE RECLUSE

China has had many hermit poets who chose to retire from public life and contemplate a higher truth in nature. The most revered of these is T'ao Yüan-ming, often referred to as the "Father of Eremitic Poetry." Also known as T'ao Ch'ien (A.D. 372–427), he lived at a time of great political unrest. Chinese historians call this the Period of Travail (A.D. 222–618). The northern provinces were being invaded by barbarians, and the southern provinces, where T'ao lived, were ruled by a series of weak and ineffective dynasties. It was a time when government positions were coveted and then abused for personal gain. T'ao Yüan-ming's great grandfather had served as minister of war, and his father and grandfather were both magistrates. Even his wife's father was a general. But still the family was poor, attesting to their refusal to participate in corruption. The poet grew up believing in the Confucian ideal of public service, and he tried several official posts, finally obtaining an appointment as magistrate. He only served for eighty-three days, however, before retiring, at the age of thirty-three, to a farming village near Mount Lu in what is now Kiangsi province. In his words, "Hunger and cold can cause physical suffering, but to do things against my conscience ... tortures my spirit." He preferred simple, rustic joys and writing about the shadow-play of life.

T'ao Yüan-ming's poetry brought two new elements to

the poetic tradition. He described nature intimately, using plain, unaffected words rather than creating images with evocative and colorful symbols. And he wrote about children. He had five sons and they were among his favorite topics, along with drinking wine (referred to as "the thing in the cup"), and chrysanthemums, a flower that became associated with his name for fifteen hundred years. He was even known as the "poet of the old people" because he wrote of passing years and he painted chrysanthemums, a flower that grows in the fall and symbolizes approaching old age, in thin, light colors.

T'ao Yüan-ming's poetry is filled with the paradoxes he felt: a love of the country and family life but a vague longing for the past; a desire for public service but anger against political corruption; and spiritual enlightenment with a moody fear of death. His spirit was Taoist, his poetry meditative, expressing views of "cloudy serenity." In fact, clouds symbolize recluse poets and are often found in their poetry. The Taoist mystique offered spiritual sustenance to all for whom the times were out of joint; T'ao Yüan-ming embraced it.

Another well-known eremitic poet, epitomizing the image of the "ragged hermit" for centuries to come, was Han-shan. Little is known about the poet himself, but his Cold Mountain Poems reveal a detachment from human comforts and a disarming joy in nature. Han-shan lived during the great T'ang dynasty; his dates are roughly ascribed to A.D. 700-780. He and his sidekick Shih-te, a cook at a nearby Temple, were thought to be incarnations of bodhisattvas, men who have attained enlightenment, according to local Buddhist monks. The governor of the prefecture described Han-shan as a "tramp" and "a crazy character." "His body and face were old and beat.... His hat was made of birch bark, his clothes were ragged and worn out, and his shoes were wood." Believing the two were holy men acting as madmen, the governor ordered the monks to collect the poems "written on bamboo, wood, stones, and cliffs—and ... on the walls of people's houses."* There were more than 300 and they were put together in a book.

Most of the poems in the collection appear to be by one man, Han-shan, presumably a poor farmer, perhaps a minor official, who became disillusioned with the ways of men and retired to live in a mountain wilderness. The poems are about Cold Mountain as a place, located in the mountain range of Mount T'ien-t'ai along the northeastern border of what is now Chekiang province; and, in the Buddhist interpretation, Cold Mountain is a state of mind, a mystical place within the heart, an inner peace sought by men. The selection of Cold Mountain poems here presents the hermit in his search for spirituality, his moods of elation and despair, and his fresh perceptions of a place of exceptional natural beauty.

---

*From the Preface to *The Poems of Han-shan*, translated by Gary Snyder.

MATCHING A POEM BY SECRETARY KUO

T'AO YÜAN-MING

Thick thick the woods before my hall,
in midsummer storing up clear shade;
southwinds come in season,
gusts flapping open the breast of my robe.
Done with friends, I pass the time in idle studies,
out of bed, fondling books and lute;
garden vegetables with flavor to spare,
last year's grain that goes a little farther—
there's a limit to what you need;
more than enough would be no cause for joy.
I pound grain to make good wine,
ferment and ladle it myself.
The little boys play by my side,
learning words they can't pronounce—
true happiness lies in these,
official hatpins all but forgotten.
Far far off I watch the white clouds,
my longing for the past deeper than words.

(Translated by Burton Watson)

BLAMING SONS

T'AO YÜAN-MING

White hair shrouds both my temples,
my skin and flesh have lost their fullness.
Though I have five male children,
not a one of them loves brush and paper.
A-shu's already twice times eight—
in laziness he's never been rivaled.
A-hsuan's going on fifteen
but cares nothing for letters or learning.
Yung and Tuan are thirteen
and can't tell a 6 from a 7!
T'ung-tzu's approaching age nine—
all he does is hunt for chestnuts and pears.
If this is the luck Heaven sends me,
then pour me the "thing in the cup"!

(Translated by Burton Watson)

WRITTEN WHILE DRUNK

T'AO YÜAN-MING

I built my house near where others dwell,
And yet there is no clamour of carriages and horses.
You ask of me "How can this be so?"
"When the heart is far the place of itself is distant."
I pluck chrysanthemums under the eastern hedge,
And gaze afar towards the southern mountains.
The mountain air is fine at evening of the day
And flying birds return together homewards.
Within these things there is a hint of Truth,
But when I start to tell it, I cannot find the words.

(Translated by Cyril Birch)

CHINESE POETRY

COLD MOUNTAIN POEMS

HAN-SHAN

The path to Han-shan's place is laughable,
A path, but no sign of cart or horse.
Converging gorges—hard to trace their twists
Jumbled cliffs—unbelievably rugged.
A thousand grasses bend with dew,
A hill of pines hums in the wind.
And now I've lost the shortcut home,
Body asking shadow, how do you keep up?

In the mountains it's cold.
Always been cold, not just this year.
Jagged scarps forever snowed in
Woods in the dark ravines spitting mist.
Grass is still sprouting at the end of June,
Leaves begin to fall in early August.
And here am I, high on mountains,
Peering and peering, but I can't even see the sky.

I wanted a good place to settle:
Cold Mountain would be safe.
Light wind in a hidden pine—
Listen close—the sound gets better.
Under it a gray-haired man
Mumbles along reading Huang and Lao.
For ten years I haven't gone back home
I've even forgotten the way by which I came.

In my first thirty years of life
I roamed hundreds and thousands of miles.

Entered cities of boiling red dust.
Tried drugs, but couldn't make Immortal;
Read books and wrote poems on history.
Today I'm back at Cold Mountain:
I'll sleep by the creek and purify my ears.

Men ask the way to Cold Mountain.
Cold Mountain: there's no through trail.
In summer, ice doesn't melt
The rising sun blurs in swirling fog.
How did I make it?
My heart's not the same as yours.
If your heart was like mine
You'd get it and be right here.

Clambering up the Cold Mountain path,
The Cold Mountain trail goes on and on:
The long gorge choked with scree and boulders,
The wide creek, the mist-blurred grass.
The moss is slippery, though there's been no rain
The pine sings, but there's no wind.
Who can leap the world's ties
And sit with me among the white clouds?

I have lived at Cold Mountain
These thirty long years.
Yesterday I called on friends and family:
More than half had gone to the Yellow Springs.
Slowly consumed, like fire down a candle;
Forever flowing, like a passing river.
Now, morning, I face my lone shadow:
Suddenly my eyes are bleared with tears.

Cold Mountain is a house
Without beams or walls.
The six doors left and right are open
The hall is blue sky.
The rooms all vacant and vague
The east wall beats on the west wall
At the center nothing.

Once more at Cold Mountain, troubles cease—
No more tangled, hung-up mind.
I idly scribble poems on the rock cliff,
Taking whatever comes, like a drifting boat.

I've lived at Cold Mountain—how many autumns.
Alone, I hum a song—utterly without regret.
Hungry, I eat one grain of Immortal-medicine
Mind solid and sharp; leaning on a stone.

Spring-water in the green creek is clear
Moonlight on Cold Mountain is white
Silent knowledge—the spirit is enlightened of itself
Contemplate the void: this world exceeds stillness.

(Translated by Gary Snyder)

FOUR

FAMOUS T'ANG DYNASTY POETS

The T'ang dynasty (A.D. 618–906) is considered China's "Golden Age of Poetry," producing her most famous poets and what has been admired as the most technically pure poetic expressions. The dynasty blossomed under the enlightened Emperor T'ai Tsung, who reigned for twenty-two years and set the scene for art and culture to become China's most treasured assets. He elevated the roles of scholar and poet to high ranks and founded the Academy of Ch'ang-an in 630. The capital city of Ch'ang-an was a symbol of opulence—the pinnacle of material, cultural, and intellectual civilization known at the time. Goods and merchants from Central Asia and other lands flowed into the city, and all art forms flourished, including the opening of a drama school. His son, Emperor Kao Tsung, succeeded him in 635 and reigned for thirty-four years. Gradually corruption began to rot away the foundation of the empire and the decline became official with the An Lu-shan rebellion of 755. The glory of the T'ang was never restored. But during the "Golden Days," poetry was prince, and China's best-loved poets were born into a nourishing environment.

Tu Fu (712–770), descended from a generation of scholars, is generally considered China's greatest poet. He achieved a perfection of condensed meaning—parallel images of the natural world and the human condition—that has been unrivaled. Because of this quality, and the packed nature of the Chinese character, translators have found Tu Fu's poetry the most difficult to render into few poetic English words. He took his role as poet seriously, following the Confucian code of duty, and worked hard at using innovative language—adding time, events, dialogue—to perfect his messages. One line of his poetry fills the reader with an explosion of meaning, as in these most famous six words: *"Blue* is the *smoke* of *war, white* the *bones* of *men."* Although his poetic genius was not recognized until some time later, he is beloved among the Chinese because of his deep pathos and sympathy with the common people. His poems are intensely personal, and he became well-known in his lifetime, wandering throughout the provinces, seeing, feeling, and capturing in poetry the whole glory and decadence of the T'ang dynasty: the glitter of court rituals, the warmth of family and friends, the beauty of nature, and the tragedy and suffering of war and famine.

At one point Tu Fu fled the T'ang capital of Ch'ang-an with his family, but he was captured by rebel armies and imprisoned for ten months. He never regained a position of favor. He had a brief respite from his wanderings and lived quietly in a cottage in Ch'eng-tu, Szechuan province. When his benefactor died, Tu Fu assumed his "eternal wanderer" role one last time, for five years, as a white-haired old man. He journeyed down the Yangtze River toward his old home in the eastern region of Lo-yang, but never arrived there. Lost in a boat in a storm, he took refuge in an abandoned temple and was near death when townspeople found him. He ate and drank at a feast in his honor, but was found dead in his bed the next morning. He was fifty-nine.

Li Po (701–762), a contemporary and friend of Tu Fu,

was a Taoist poet from Szechuan province. He claimed royal ancestry, but more likely, as legend has it, his ancestors were marauding murderers and thieves. Tall and powerfully built, Li Po ate and drank copiously, married three times, insulted whomever he pleased, behaved irreverently as a drunkard and rogue, and was exiled twice, arrested three times, and even sentenced to death once.

Li Po's poetry—impersonal, imaginative, playful—is full of life and colors, celebrating women, nature, and friendship, but never death. He was troubled by the impermanence of beauty and often included an element of mystery or screening in his poems. But he reveled in the image of the creative, irresponsible poet. He was a showman and would dress up in garments made of flowers—his black, long hair loose and flowing down his shoulders, his black eyes raging with an insatiable hunger—and he would recite his poems deliriously, as though possessed by the gods. In contrast to Tu Fu, he composed poetry effortlessly, in the old styles, delighting in making his poems into paper boats and sailing them down a stream. Only a small portion of his poems survived. Incorrigible, but gifted in perceiving and expressing the wonders of life, Li Po has been called "the spirit of freedom walking in a bloody land."

The traditional account of his death is that while drunk he tried to kiss his reflection in the moonlit river, fell in, and drowned. Older than Tu Fu by about ten years, he died before his friend, at the age of sixty-one.

Po Chü-i (772–846) was a precocious child, surviving a childhood of poverty in Honan and graduating as *chin-shih* (advanced scholar) at the age of seventeen. He lived well, rising to high official ranks during the second half of the T'ang dynasty and enjoying his fame as a poet by the age of thirty. His poems were sung by plowboys and court dancers, inscribed on walls in temples and schools, and recited by emperors. Later in life he preserved all twenty-eight hundred of his poems in volumes which he distributed to his children and libraries.

His most famous poem, "The Everlasting Sorrow," tells of Emperor Ming Huang and his passionate love for a beautiful consort, Yang Kuei-fei. The poem recounts his flight from the palace and her death for treason at the hands of his own soldiers:

> The Emperor could not save her, he could only cover his face.
> And later when he turned to look, the place of blood and tears
> Was hidden in a yellow dust blown by a cold wind.

Grief-stricken, the Emperor seeks out a Taoist monk who "could by his faith summon the spirits from the dead." Yang Kuei-fei is found in a palace on "five-colored clouds" and sends back a gold hairpin and inlaid case as keepsakes of her love, promising that they will meet again.

> "On the Seventh day of the Seventh month, in the Palace of Long Life,
> We told each other secretly in the quiet midnight world
> That we wished to fly in heaven, two birds with the wings of one,
> And to grow together on the earth, two branches of one tree."
> ... Earth endures, heaven endures; some time both shall end,
> While this unending sorrow goes on and on for ever.*

*From a translation of the poem by Witter Bynner.

Po Chü-i's poems are simple and exact, easily translated and accessible, often filled with passion for the moment, seldom signifying anything timeless or eternal. For this reason Po is widely quoted. He wrote about social justice, quiet pleasures, and sorrow. Some of his poetry is melancholy, brought on by frequent separations from a lifelong friendship with the poet Yuan Chen. Strongly Confucian and idealist, there are didactic elements in his verse, illustrating his view that poetry should serve society, not art.

RESTLESS NIGHT

TU FU

The cool of bamboo invades my room;
moonlight from the fields fills the corners of the court;
dew gathers till it falls in drops;
a scattering of stars, now there, now gone.
A firefly threading the darkness makes his own light;
birds at rest on the water call to each other;
all these lie within the shadow of the sword—
Powerless I grieve as the clear night passes.

(Translated by Burton Watson)

TO LI PO AT THE SKY'S END

TU FU

A cold wind blows from the far sky....
What are you thinking of, old friend?
The wildgeese never answer me.
Rivers and lakes are flooded with rain.
... A poet should beware of prosperity,
Yet demons can haunt a wanderer.
Ask an unhappy ghost, throw poems to him
Where he drowned himself in the Milo River.*

(Translated by Witter Bynner)

*Reference to the poet Ch'ü Yüan.

JADE FLOWER PALACE

TU FU

The stream swirls. The wind moans in
The pines. Grey rats scurry over
Broken tiles. What prince, long ago,
Built this palace, standing in
Ruins beside the cliffs? There are
Green ghost fires in the black rooms.
The shattered pavements are all
Washed away. Ten thousand organ
Pipes whistle and roar. The storm
Scatters the red autumn leaves.
His dancing girls are yellow dust.
Their painted cheeks have crumbled
Away. His gold chariots
And courtiers are gone. Only
A stone horse is left of his
Glory. I sit on the grass and
Start a poem, but the pathos of
It overcomes me. The future
Slips imperceptibly away.
Who can say what the years will bring?

(Translated by Kenneth Rexroth)

A TRAVELER AT NIGHT WRITES HIS THOUGHTS

TU FU

Delicate grasses, faint wind on the bank;
Stark mask, a long night boat:
Stars hang down, over broad fields sweeping;
The moon boils up, on the great river flowing.
Fame—how can my writings win me that?
Office—age and sickness have brought it to an end.
Fluttering, fluttering—where is my likeness?
Sky and earth and one sandy gull.

(Translated by Burton Watson)

ON THE MOUNTAIN: QUESTION AND ANSWER

LI PO

You ask me
            Why do I live
on this green mountain?
       I smile
       No answer
            My heart serene
On flowing water
              peachblow
              quietly going
              far away
          another earth
This is   another sky
No likeness
          to that human world below

(Translated by C. H. Kwock and Vincent McHugh)

A YELLOW CRANE TOWER SEEING OFF MENG HAU-RAN ON HIS WAY TO YANG-JOU

LI PO

My old friend
Bids farewell to me
In the west at Yellow Crane Tower.
Amid April's mist and flowers
He goes down to Yang-jou.

The distant image
Of his lonely sail
Disappears in blue emptiness,
And all I see
Is the Long River
Flowing to the edge of the sky.

(Translated by Greg Whincup)

DRINKING ALONE IN THE MOONLIGHT

LI PO

A pot of wine among flowers.
I alone, drinking, without a companion.
I lift the cup and invite the bright moon.
My shadow opposite certainly makes us three.
But the moon cannot drink,
And my shadow follows the motions of my body in vain.
For the briefest time are the moon and my shadow my companions.
Oh, be joyful! One must make the most of Spring.
I sing—the moon walks forward rhythmically;
I dance, and my shadow shatters and becomes confused.
In my waking moments, we are happily blended.
When I am drunk, we are divided from one another and scattered.
For a long time I shall be obligated to wander without intention.
But we will keep our appointment by the far-off Cloudy River.

(Translated by Florence Ayscough and Amy Lowell)

TOO BRILLIANT

PO CH'Ü-I

From distant Annam there came a gift—
a scarlet parrot with coloured plumage
like peach blossom; so clever that
it could speak like men;

    so, as with clever men
    they put it in a cage
    where it sits wondering
    when it shall taste of life again.

(Translated by Rewi Alley)

BITTER COLD, LIVING IN THE VILLAGE

PO CHÜ—I

In the twelfth month of the Eighth Year,
On the fifth day, a heavy snow fell.
Bamboos and cypress all perished from the freeze.
How much worse for people without warm clothes!

As I looked around the village,
Of ten families, eight or nine were in need.
The north wind was sharper than the sword,
And homespun cloth could hardly cover one's body.
Only brambles were burnt for firewood,
And sadly people sat at night to wait for dawn.

From this I know that when winter is harsh,
The farmers suffer most.
Looking at myself, during these days—
How I'd shut tight the gate of my thatched hall,
Cover myself with fur, wool, and silk,
Sitting or lying down, I had ample warmth.
I was lucky to be spared cold or hunger,
Neither did I have to labor in the field.

Thinking of that, how can I not feel ashamed?
I ask myself what kind of man am I.

(Translated by Irving Y. Lo)

THE POEM ON THE WALL*

PO CH'Ü-I

My clumsy poem on the inn-wall none cared to see.
With bird-droppings and moss's growth the letters were blotched away.
There came a guest with heart so full, that though a page to the Throne,
He did not grudge with his broidered coat to wipe off the dust, and read.

(Translated by Arthur Waley)

---

*Yuan Chen wrote that on his way to exile he had discovered a poem inscribed by Po Chü-i on the wall of an inn.

FIVE

CHINESE WOMEN AND POETRY

Throughout Chinese literature women receive great attention. They are exalted as beautiful objects, condemned as wicked tricksters, and occasionally lamented as poignant, tragic casualties in a man's world. In fact, the figure of a lonely, beautiful woman longing for her mate became an obsession for Chinese poets over the centuries. Regardless of this lofty focus, however, a woman's place in Chinese society was severely restricted since the earliest times. And philosophical writings left no doubt as to the proper role for females. An old proverb says it all: "A woman's virtue lies in her ignorance." Born without status, trained as domestic and sexual slaves, isolated emotionally, and restricted physically (foot binding began in the tenth century as a way of confining women to the home), women who achieved any level of political influence or literary accomplishment were rare indeed.

Two women writers—Pan Chao and Ts'ai Wen-chi—are mentioned in the histories of the Han dynasty. Ts'ai Yen (second century A.D.) is traditionally acknowledged as the first notable woman poet in Chinese history. And two T'ang poetesses, a courtesan and a nun, were acknowledged, even though their poetry was not considered meritorious. However, two women left lasting marks on China's most famous literary scene during the T'ang dynasty. The wife of Emperor T'ai Tsung, a ruler dedicated to the cultural esteem of his empire, convinced her husband to build a library as part of the newly founded Academy of Ch'ang in 630, instead of spending the money on an extravagant tomb for her. And Empress Wu, a former nun who gained control of her empire after the death of her husband, made poetry compulsory in public examinations, along with Confucian and Taoist thought, in 690.

But, according to another proverb, "Many men can build a state, but it takes only one woman to destroy it." So poor Yang Kuei-fei, beautiful consort of Emperor Ming Huang (immortalized in the poem "Everlasting Sorrow" by Po Chü-i), was credited with "poisoning" the T'ang court and singlehandedly destroying the empire. She was hanged for treason in 755 for plotting with the rebel An Lu-shan who marched on the capital, resulting in the loss of twelve million lives, civil war, and destruction of the glorious T'ang empire!

It wasn't until the Sung dynasty that a woman poet, Li Ch'ing-chao (A.D. 1083–1149), was recognized as a literary artist equal to her male contemporaries. She remains today China's most famous poetess. Born into an aristocratic family and married to a scholar, Li and her husband spent a lifetime preserving manuscripts and collecting books and calligraphic works (nearly twenty thousand volumes, most of which were lost or destroyed during the Chin invasion). The bulk of her poetry was composed after the death of her husband, which occurred when she was forty-seven. Once a woman became too old to be a sexual commodity, she gained more freedom; this appears to be so with Li Ch'ing-chao and many other women poets. Another well-known Sung woman poet, Chu Shu-chên, unhappy in her marriage, is a vivid portrait of the forlorn lady. Embarrassed by her open expressions, and to preserve the family reputation, her parents burned most of her poetry after her death.

Most women in China, however, led lives of quiet desperation. The great majority became wives: "Unmarried, she owed obedience to her father; married, to her husband; in widowhood, to her sons." Those who were not fortunate enough to marry had very few options: to live as a concubine to an emperor or chieftain; to entertain men as a singing girl or courtesan (prostitutes in China often wielded much influence); or to become a matchmaker, herbalist, or midwife. Buddhist nuns and Taoist priestesses were involved in scholarly pursuits and allowed to become literate, along with courtesans, who were prolific in writing folk songs. Although women did not hold official positions, nor were they allowed to take the imperial examinations, many women poets were well versed in politics, religion, and sex. In fact, Taoist priestesses were in great demand as sexual teachers, and much of the eroticism found in Chinese poetry comes from women.

The poems here, by women (and by men about women) up to the eighteenth century, are full of human emotion. Although women poets wrote about many subjects—friendship, travel, nature—most of their poems are about love and loneliness. Some male poets, notably Li Po and Su Tung-p'o, wrote in the persona of a disconsolate woman. But nearly all poets wrote about women. A few selections from the *Book of Songs* appear to be by women, but authorship there is uncertain. Unfortunately, there appears to be virtually no poetry written by women about the home, children, and motherhood.

WOMAN

FU HSUAN, 3RD CENTURY A.D.

How sad it is to be a woman!
Nothing on earth is held so cheap.
Boys standing leaning at the door
Like Gods fallen out of Heaven.
Their hearts brave the Four Oceans,
The wind and dust of a thousand miles.
No one is glad when a girl is born;
By her the family sets no store.
When she grows up, she hides in her room
Afraid to look a man in the face.
No one cries when she leaves her home—
Sudden as clouds when the rain stops.
She bows her head and composes her face,
Her teeth are pressed on her red lips:
She bows and kneels countless times.
She must humble herself even to the servants.
His love is distant as the stars in Heaven,
Yet the sunflower bends toward the sun.
Their hearts more sundered than water and fire—
A hundred evils are heaped upon her.
Her face will follow the years' changes;
Her lord will find new pleasures.
They that were once like substances and shadow
Are now as far as Hu from Ch'in.*
Yet Hu and Ch'in shall sooner meet
Than they whose parting is like Ts'an and Ch'en.**

(Translated by Arthur Waley)

---

*Two lands.
**Two stars.

FOLK SONG

ANONYMOUS

Black ravens squawking in the nest.
Everybody says I have too many sisters.
Ten aren't many.
First sister marries a carpenter.
Wooden beams hold up the roof.
Second marries a bamboo cutter.
Our wet clothes dry on poles.
Third sister marries a fisherman.
Fish, shrimp and crabs go in the soup.
Fourth sister marries a weaver.
We're wearing silk and satin.
Fifth one marries a beancake man.
Starch the clothes in soybean milk.
Sixth sister marries a butcher.
Bean paste fries in lard.
Seventh marries a painter.
The table's painted, the bed's red.
Eighth sister marries a watchman.
Every night he drums you to bed.
Ninth sister marries a tailor.
Measures us for a dress.
Tenth sister marries a farmer.
Piles of rice,
piles of wood,
piles of husks.

(Translated by Cecelia Liang)

LOVELY THE YOUNG PEACH TREE

ANONYMOUS, CIRCA 600 B.C.

Lovely the young peach tree,
    Shimmering its blossoms.
This girl goes to a new home
    To order well its chambers.

Lovely the young peach tree,
    Plentiful its fruit.
This girl goes to a new home
    To order well its rooms.

Lovely the young peach tree,
    Rich its leaves.
This girl goes to a new home
    To order well its people.

(Translated by Burton Watson)

THE BOAT OF CYPRESS WOOD

ANONYMOUS, CIRCA 600 B.C.

Freely floats the boat of cypress wood,
Tossing about along the stream.
Eyes open, I can't fall asleep,
As if my heart were heavy with grief.
It's not that I've no wine to drink,
Or nowhere to enjoy visiting.

My heart's not like a bronze mirror,
Absorbing the reflection of everything.
I've brothers, elder and younger,
But not one is trustworthy.
When I tried to pour out my grievances,
I found them furious with me.

My heart's not like a stone,
It can't be turned and moved easily.
My heart's not like a mat,
It can't be rolled up at will.
With dignity and honour,
I'll never flinch or yield.

My heart's weighed down with vexation,
Against me the villains bear a grudge.
Excessive distress I've been confronted with,
Too much indignity I've been treated with.
Meditating silently on this,
I beat my breast when the sad truth dawns on me.

Oh sun, oh moon,
Why are you always so dim?
My heart stained with sorrow,
Cannot be washed clean like dirty clothes.
I reflect silently on this,
And cannot spread my wings and soar high.

*(Translated by Yang Xianyi,
Gladys Yang, and Hu Shiguang)*

NINETEEN OLD POEMS OF THE HAN ... #2*

MEI SHENG, 2ND CENTURY B.C.

Green green, river bank grasses,
thick thick, willows in the garden;
plump plump, that lady upstairs,
bright bright, before the window;
lovely lovely, her red face-powder;
slim slim, she puts out a white hand.
Once I was a singing-house girl,
now the wife of a wanderer,
a wanderer who never comes home—
It's hard sleeping in an empty bed alone.

(Translated by Burton Watson)

---

*One of the earliest examples of a poem written by a man assuming the persona of a woman.

JADE STAIRS RESENTMENT

LI PO, 8TH CENTURY

On steps of jade
White dew forms.
It creeps within
Her stockings of fine silk.
As night grows long.

She lowers then
The water-crystal blind,
And through its glittering gems
She gazes
At the autumn moon.

(Translated by Greg Whincup)

WILLOW EYEBROWS

CHAO LUAN-LUAN,* 8TH CENTURY

Sorrows play at the edge of these willow leaf curves.
They are often reflected, deep, deep,
In my water blossom inlaid mirror,
I am too pretty to bother with an eyebrow pencil.
Spring hills paint themselves
With their own personality.

(Translated by Kenneth Rexroth and Ling Chung)

---

*An elegant courtesan in the T'ang capital of Ch'ang-an who wrote poems in praise of the parts of a woman's body.

ON A VISIT TO CH'UNG CHEN TAOIST TEMPLE I SEE IN THE SOUTH HALL THE LIST OF SUCCESSFUL CANDIDATES IN THE IMPERIAL EXAMINATIONS

Y'Ü HS'ÜAN-CHI,* 9TH CENTURY

Cloud capped peaks fill the eyes
In the Spring sunshine.
Their names are written in beautiful characters
And posted in order of merit.
Now I hate this silk dress
That conceals a poet.
I lift my head and read their names
In powerless envy.

(Translated by Kenneth Rexroth and Ling Chung)

---

*A Taoist priestess who had many poet lovers; she was accused of murdering her maid and was executed.

TO THE TUNE "A HILLY GARDEN"

LI CH'ING-CHAO, 12TH CENTURY

Spring has come to the women's quarters.
The grass turns green.
The red buds of the plum trees have cracked
But are not yet fully open.
Blue green clouds carve jade dragons.
The jade powder becomes fine dust.
I try to hold on to my morning dream,
But I am startled by the breaking cup of Spring.

Flower shadows lie heavy on the garden gate.
A pale moon is spread on the translucent curtain
In the beautiful orange twilight.
For two years, three times, I have missed
The Lord of Spring.
Now he is coming home,
And I will thoroughly enjoy this Spring.

(Translated by Kenneth Rexroth and Ling Chung)

SPRING JOY

CHU SHU-CHÊN, 12TH CENTURY

Drafty winds and fine rain
Make a chilly Spring.
I drink wine, remembering bygone happiness,
Under the pear blossoms,
Weeping with misery.
Through the scented grasses
And broken mists, we walked
Along the Southern bank of the river,
Tears of farewell
Blurring the distant mountains.
Last night I was fulfilled in a dream.
Speechless, we made love
In mist and clouds.
Alas, when I awoke
The old agony returned.
I tossed in my quilt
Angry at my own helplessness.
It is easier to see Heaven
Than to see you.

(Translated by Kenneth Rexroth and Ling Chung)

SEEKING A MOORING

WANG WEI,* 17TH CENTURY

A leaf floats in endless space.
A cold wind tears the clouds.
The water flows westward.
The tide pushes upstream.
Beyond the moonlit reeds,
In village after village, I hear
The sound of fullers' mallets
Beating the wet clothing
In preparation for winter.
Everywhere crickets cry
In the autumn frost.
A traveller's thoughts in the night
Wander in a thousand miles of dreams.
The sound of a bell cannot disperse
The sorrows that come
In the fifth hour of night.
What place will I remember
From all this journey?
Only still bands of desolate mist
And a single fishing boat.

(Translated by Kenneth Rexroth and Ling Chung)

---

*A woman poet who became a Taoist priestess after her husbands died and traveled with her library on a little boat through the waterways of Central China. The famous T'ang dynasty poet and painter Wang Wei's name has a different character for *wei*.

SIX

POETRY IN MUSIC, ART, AND THEATRE

After the T'ang dynasty Chinese art and culture continued its refinement. People traveled freely by boat, carriage, or horse on well-worn roadways and waterways; they sat on chairs, drank tea, used paper money, and read printed books; they even experimented with explosive weapons. Indeed, the capitals of the Chinese dynasties from the Sung (960–1279) into the Ch'ing (1644–1911) were among the largest and most civilized cities in the world at the time. Marco Polo visited China in 1271, returning to Europe with riches from the East, including silks, porcelains, and chinaware, as well as scrolls of brush-stroked calligraphy and landscape paintings with poems inscribed in the corners.

The T'ang dynasty had reached a high level of literary achievement in poetry primarily because of the intensely structured nature of the *shih* form. Poets worked on packing meaning through imagery into four, five, or seven characters to each line, often in rhymed couplets. This form became world-renowned and symbolic of the technical expertise of Chinese poets.

However, after centuries of imposed regularity, poets were anxious to explore new meters and patterns. The importation of music from Central Asia and other Western cultures played an influential role in new developments, as did the combined impact of Buddhism and a new wave of Confucianism that emerged from the T'ang dynasty. Poems of uneven lines offered poets more freedom of expression, and longer, narrative poems allowed them to tell stories. All poetry is personal expression, but some poetic styles were more entertaining, more social, more political. Prose ballads in the folk storytelling tradition (*fu*), some written with musical accompaniment, and song lyrics written to existing popular tunes and performed at court by female entertainers (*tz'u*) provided new models for Sung dynasty poets. Later, arias or song-poems (*ch'u*) were written for the budding Chinese theatre, and poems were written specifically as a complement to paintings. All forms, and their numerous variations, became accepted as legitimate poetry by the literati and, later, by scholars of Chinese literature.

In fact, after the T'ang dynasty spawned the great masters of the *shih*, poetry flourished in all its forms. Sung dynasty (960–1279) poets wrote copious poems in all styles, about heretofore *un*poetic subjects (animals, children, everyday affairs of ordinary people). The poems were often more philosophical, humanistic, and colloquial; in tone they were more carefree. Poets employed multiple metaphors instead of relying on the traditional nature symbolism. During the Yuan dynasty (1279–1368), when the Mongols were in power and many scholar-officials and poets protested the foreign rule, and the Ming dynasty (1368–1644), when fiction and drama developed as predominant literary forms, poetry was incorporated into other art forms. In fact, it appears that artists of the times were seeking one integrated art form which would satisfy them all. Painter-poets, dramatist-poets, calligraphers, and musician-poets merged their art forms in deliberate attempts to create new styles from the old, orthodox methods of the earlier masters. To be an artist at this time was a fine ambition among young men in the educated classes.

Notable among Chinese artists in this era of integrated forms were Wang Wei (701-761), the most famous painter-poet—known for the "painting in his poetry and the poetry in his painting,"—and Su T'ung-po (1037-1101), master of the *tz'u* lyric form, as well as a painter of some distinction. Shen Chou (1427-1509) was one of China's greatest landscape painters, and Chu Yün-ming (1461-1527) is recognized as one of the most important masters of Chinese calligraphy; both have poems represented here. The other verses selected illustrate the wide range of styles, subjects, and techniques used by most poets of the period.

COMPOSED ON A SPRING DAY ON THE FARM

WANG WEI, 8TH CENTURY

Spring pigeons bill and coo under the rocks;
Returning swallows spy out their former nests;
Apricot blossoms whiten the outskirts of the village.
Axes in hand, the peasants set out to prune the mulberry trees,
Or shouldering hoes, explore water sources for irrigation.
Old people leaf over the latest almanac.
As for me, with my cup of wine, I suddenly forget to drink,
Whelmed in abysmal longing for friends far away.

(Translated by Chang Yin-nan and Lewis C. Walmsley)

IN A BOAT, GETTING UP AT NIGHT

SU T'UNG-PO, 11TH CENTURY

A gentle breeze rustles through reeds and rushes—
I open the hatch to watch the rain, as moonlight floods the lake.
Boatmen and waterfowls share alike the same dream;
Big fish, startled, speed away like scurrying foxes.
Late at night, men and objects do not feel for one another;
I alone am amused by things and their shadows.
Tides rising unseen from the bank, I mourn the wintry earthworms;
A setting moon caught by the willows, I watch a spider strung.
This fleeting life spent in sickness and worry—
The pure vision passes before my eyes just for a moment.
When cocks crow and bells sound, flocks of birds scatter—
Soon the drum beats at the prow and people call to one another.

(Translated by Irving Yucheng Lo)

THE DAPPLED HORSE

MEI YAO-CH'EN, 11TH CENTURY

The boat moored, lunch in a lonely village;
on the far bank I see a dappled horse,
in lean pasture, gaunt with hunger;
scruffy birds flocking down to peck his feed.
Pity is powerless—I have no bow;
again and again I try to pelt them with clods
but I haven't the strength to manage a hit,
face sweaty and hot with chagrin.

(Translated by Burton Watson)

FARM FAMILIES

LU YU, 12TH CENTURY

It's late, the children come home from school;
braids unplaited, they ramble the fields,
jeering at each other—guess what's in my hand!
arguing—who won the grass fight after all?
Father sternly calls them to lessons;
grandfather indulgently feeds them candy.
We don't ask you to become rich and famous,
but when the time comes, work hard in the fields!

(Translated by Burton Watson)

SENDING OFF SPRING

KUAN YÜN-SHIH, 14TH CENTURY

Ask the Lord of the East*, "Where lie the ends of the earth?"
Setting sun and singing cuckoos,
Flowing water and peach blossoms,
Dim, dim distant mountains,
Lush, lush fragrant grasses,
Dark, dark red sunset clouds.
Pursue willow catkins and where would the wind transport you?
Chase floating spider silk and to whose house would you be enticed?
Languidly tuning a balloon lute
She leans on the swing,
The window gauze reflecting moonlight.

(Translated by Richard John Lynn)

---

*The god of spring.

TO THE TUNE "NAN-HSIANG-TZU"

EXPRESSING MY FEELINGS

SHEN CHOU, 15TH CENTURY

I'm a mad immortal between heaven and earth,
painting pictures, writing poems,
> but never to sell for cash!
Pictures—in debt! Poems—unpaid taxes!
> Busy until old age.
What a shame . . .
Friendships, feelings for people, all have led to nothing.

This has been the worst year of all:
waves pounding the thatched walls,
> river flooding the fields.
I'd better pick up my brush and inkstone
and—say no more!
move my home on board a fishing boat.

(Translated by Jonathan Chaves)

CHINESE POETRY

A LADY PICKING FLOWERS

SHEN CHOU, 15TH CENTURY

Last year we parted as the flowers began to bloom.
Now the flowers bloom again, and you still have not
 returned.
Purple grief, red sorrow—a hundred thousand kinds,
and the spring wind blows each of them into my hands.

(Translated by Jonathan Chaves)

A PAINTING OF THE BUTTERFLY DREAM BY THE MASTER ARTIST LI TSAI

CHU YÜN-MING, 15TH CENTURY

I used to dream of Chuang Tzu;*
I read every word in his book.
Day and night I thought of meeting him,
"flitting and fluttering" before my eyes!
But Chuang Tzu cannot come back,
the butterfly cannot appear again:
so who put them into this painting?
I see them and feel we're old friends!
If Chuang Tzu could become a butterfly,
why shouldn't a butterfly be able to become me?
The dream of a thousand years, here on this paper—
how do I know it is not my own?

(Translated by Jonathan Chaves)

---

*Taoist philosopher who dreamed he was a butterfly, and when he awoke, could not decide if he was a man dreaming he was a butterfly or a butterfly dreaming he was a man.

TO THE TUNE "RED EMBROIDERED SHOES"

HUANG O, 16TH CENTURY

If you don't know how, why pretend?
Maybe you can fool some girls,
But you can't fool Heaven.
I dreamed you'd play with the
Locust blossom under my green jacket,
Like a eunuch with a courtesan.
But lo and behold!
All you can do is mumble.
You've made me all wet and slippery,
But no matter how hard you try
Nothing happens. So stop.
Go and make somebody else
Unsatisfied.

(Translated by Kenneth Rexroth and Ling Chung)

CHINESE POETRY

FOR CONTEMPORARY ARTIST PIEN WEI-CH'I

CHENG HSIEH, 18TH CENTURY

You paint the wild geese as if I could see them crying,
And on this double-threaded silk, the rustling sound of river reeds.
On the tip of your brush, how infinitely chill is the autumn wind;
Everywhere on the mountain pass is the sorrow of parting.

(Translated by Irving Yucheng Lo)

FINDING SERENITY

YÜAN MEI, 18TH CENTURY

1.
This spring, the sky is leaking,
> clouds hang thick and heavy;
We'll have one day of deceptive clearing,
> then ten days of cloud.
Tree after tree of crab-apple flowers,
> weeping tears of red:
They seem to be lamenting to us,
> "This rain is hard to take!"

2.
In old age, life's affairs
> are supposed to leave one at peace;
how could I foresee that every morning
> as soon as I awake, there's grief?
Requests for inscriptions, calls for forewords,
> poems to be written on paintings:
busy as ever in the world of men,
> I coldly meet their requests.

3.
Setting brush to paper has always been hard
> because I want perfection:
each poem I'll change a thousand times
> before I'm content.
The matron it seems continues to act
> like an adolescent girl—
until her hair is perfectly combed
> no one's allowed to look.

4.
In snow and mud the goose leaves prints
      then flies off hurriedly:
catching sight, it's hard to keep
      my old eyes from reddening.
A letter from my family, written sixty years past,
suddenly falls floating from the pages of my book.

5.
Become an immortal! Become a Buddha?
      —It's all so hard to tell!
I'll just go and transform again
      in the Creator's furnace.
But if I do appear before the Emperor of Jade,
I'll ask, "Now, really, beyond the sky,
      is there another sky?"

(Translated by Jonathan Chaves)

SEVEN

MODERN VIEWS AND VOICES

佔

Buddhist priests from India brought new religious ideas into China at the same time Christianity developed in the Mediterranean; Taoism and Confucianism made way. The Chinese had started building the Great Wall around 200 B.C. to rebuff nomads from the north, but her boundaries were too broad to protect and her people too many to govern well. Wars among feudal lords and against attacking foreigners were common. Mongolian leader Genghis Khan conquered the northern regions and ruled China for a hundred years after the Sung dynasty. Soon after Marco Polo's visit in 1271, the Portuguese were knocking at the gate, leading a legion of European traders with profit motives and imperialist designs. The Japanese and Russians joined in the fray and China—under the rule of yet another non-native clan, the Manchus—was invaded and violated unmercifully during the nineteenth century. By the time the Chinese regained control of their country in 1911, China had been ravaged by internal and external conflict, and humiliated into social, educational, and government reforms. Dr. Sun Yat-sen struggled to lead his country into the new century and there was a brief decade or two of "modernization" in all aspects of life.

The arts that were so highly prized by traders had lost their originality and become imitations. The old culture stank of phony elitism, as corrupt as the decayed Manchu court.

All traditions were suspect, and China was angry at the intrusion. In the words of one poet:

> 1840—
> an unforgettable year
> coming in with opium,
> pirates, imperialism—
> ta madi!
> > one
> > two
> > three
> > four
>
> England, France, Japan, America;
> > they kicked open
> > the door of China*

As before, the poetry reflected these changes—in style and content—but poets, elevated in social position since the Golden Age of the T'ang, were still members of an elite literati. From the time of Confucius, literature had been preserved in a classical language, a system of calligraphy that required formal education afforded to only a small percentage of the population. This language was very different from the spoken words of the masses; therefore, even though poetry was sung in the fields and public houses and scribbled on walls and temples, only intellectuals *studied* poetry. By the end of the tumultuous nineteenth century, Chinese writers were traveling abroad, learning of the teachings of the Western world. They returned to China with new inspiration, new styles, and democratic ideas about audiences. The

---

*From "For Peace" by Li Tien-min.

most dramatic change that occurred early in the twentieth century was a change to the vernacular, or *pai-hua*. Dr. Hu Shih was a leader in this literary reform movement, and though more diplomat and scholar than poet, his poem "Old Dream" acknowledges the mixed feelings experienced during this brief resurgence of the expressive arts under China's First Republic.

Instead of merging art forms and experimenting with new variations of old poetic forms, the modern poets developed their own unique styles: Hsü Chih-mo, a singer, became a master at lyrical lines; Wen I-to, a painter, wrote with strong, vibrant, visual images; Ping Hsin, a woman sensitive to themes for young people, created flowing poems in the new vernacular; Feng Chih, a student of Rilke and Goethe, adapted the sonnet form; Ai Ch'ing, after Whitman's style, developed a sparse, rhymeless verse full of intense feelings and powerful images; and T'ien Chien, influenced by Russian poets, initiated a drumbeat verse which scholars claim restored some of the primitive spirit of the early songs to Chinese poetry.

The changes in language and style characterize the poetry of this modern period, but perhaps more significant is the emergence of a collective consciousness, a sense of patriotism for China, her people, and her stubborn, ancient soil. Foreign references reflect back to the homeland; traditional nature images mingle with blood and tears and sacrifice for a people trying to maintain their imprint in a reckless, hungry world. There is little nostalgia or longing, parting sorrow, or personal anguish over lost loved ones. This poetry speaks to a wider audience in voices that can now be understood, and it speaks about a nationalism that China had never known.

NEW YEAR'S EVE

LIU E*, 1906

The north wind blows, cracking the earth,
in sadness, seeing off the old year.
The servant announces we're out of rice,
and a creditor has come, asking for money.
A hungry crow caws in evening snow;
a wild goose cuts through cold mist.
This is the way my life is now:
others are even worse off.

(Translated by Jonathan Chaves)

---

*Considered by many scholars to be the last great practitioner of traditional *Shih* poetry.

IMPRESSIONS OF SHANGHAI

KUO MO-JO*, 1919

I was shocked out of my dream!
    Ah, the sorrow of disillusion!

Idle bodies,
    Sensual and noisy flesh,
Men wearing long robes,
    Women, short sleeves,
Everywhere I see skeletons,
    And everywhere, coffins
Madly rushing,
    Madly pushing
Tears well up in my eyes,
    And nausea, in my heart.

I was shocked out of my dream.
    Ah, the sorrow of disillusion!

(Translated by Kai-yu Hsu)

---

*Became politically involved in the new Communist regime and co-edited volumes of poetry collected from the people in the communes in the 1950s.

DELIVERANCE

PING HSIN, 1923

Moonlight, clear as water,
I pace the ground under a tree
In deep, deep thought.
Deep in thought, I pick up a fallen twig
To tap, with a sigh, my own shadow
On the moonlit ground.

Life—
Everybody treats it as a dream,
A blurred dream.
My friend,
As you try to find clear lines in the blurred world,
Your life's suffering
Thus begins!

You may treasure life's snow-white robe,
Yet life has to cross
The immense sea of darkness.
My friend,
The world does not abandon you,
Why should you abandon the world?

Let life stand alone and noble like a stork,
Free as a cloud,
And pure and calm as water,
Even if life were a dream,
Let it be a clear dream.

In deep, deep thought—
Deep in thought, I throw away the fallen twig.
Quietly and calmly I gaze at my shadow
On the moonlit ground.

(Translated by Kai-yu Hsu)

THE LAST DAY

WEN I-TO, 1926

The dewdrops sob in the roof-gutters,
The green tongues of banana leaves lap at the window
　　panes.
The four white walls seem to back away from me:
I alone can not fill such a big roon.

A brazier aflame in my heart,
I quietly await a guest from afar.
I feed the fire with cobwebs, rat dung,
And snakeskins in place of split wood.

As the roosters urge time, only ashes remain;
A chilly breeze steals over to caress my mouth.
The guest is already right in front of me;
I close my eyes and follow him away.

(Translated by Kai-yu-Hsu)

OLD DREAM

HU SHIH, 1927

From the green foliage below the hill
Emerges a corner of flying roof.
It awakens an old dream, and causes
Tears to fall within me.

For it I sing a song of old,
In a tune no one understands,
Ah, I am not really singing,
Only reviewing an old dream.

(Translated by Kai-yu Hsu)

THE REBIRTH OF SPRING

HSÜ CHIH-MO, 1929

Last night
As already the night before
Spring
Took possession of Winter's dead body.

Don't you feel the yielding underfoot?
Don't you feel the mild breath at your temples?
On the branches, a wash of green,
Ripples on the pond, endlessly weaving,
And for both of us, through our limbs,
In our breast, a new kind of beating;

On your cheeks already the peach-blossom open,
And ever more keenly I gather to me
Your beauty, drink down
The bubbling of your laughter.
Don't you feel these arms of mine
Ever more insistent, demanding to hold you?
My breath homing to strike against your body
As though a myriad of fireflies swarmed to the flame?
All these, and so many more beyond the telling
Join with the eager wheeling of the birds
And hand in hand unite to hymn
The rebirth of Spring.

(Translated by Cyril Birch)

SONNET

FENG CHIH, 1941

We stand together on top of a towering mountain
Transforming ourselves into the immense sweep of view,
Into the unlimited plain in front of us,
And into the footpaths crisscrossing the plain.

Which road, which river is unconnected, and
Which wind, which cloud is without its response?
The waters and hills we've traversed
Have all been merged in our lives.

Our births, our growth, and our sorrows
Are the lone pine standing on a mountain,
Are the dense fog blanketing a city.

We follow the blowing wind and the flowing water
To become the crisscrossing paths on the plain,
To become the lives of the travelers on the paths.

(Translated by Kai-yu Hsu)

FREEDOM IS WALKING TOWARD US

T'IEN CHIEN

A sad
Nation, ah,
We must fight!
Beyond the window, in autumn,
In the field
Of Asia,
Freedom, ah,
Is walking toward us
From beyond the blood pools,
From beyond the dead bodies of our brothers—
A wild storm,
A swooping sea swallow.

(Translated by Kai-yu-Hsu)

THE NORTH

AI CH'ING

> ONE DAY
> THE POET FROM THE MONGOLIAN PLAIN
> SAID TO ME,
> "THE NORTH IS SAD."

    Yes.
The North is sad.
From beyond the frontier blow
The desert winds
Which have already scraped away the green color of life.
And the brightness of sunlight
—The expanse of ash-yellow murk
Is covered with an unpellable layer of sand—
The storm screams that rush from the horizon
Bring with them terror
Madly
Sweeping over the wide earth;
The desert wilderness
Is frozen in the cold wind of December,
The villages, the hillsides, the river banks,
The dilapidated walls and deserted graves,
All wear the melancholy of the color of the earth . . .
A lone traveler
Body bent forward
Shading his face with his hand
In the wind and sand
Breathes with difficulty
Step by step
Struggles forward . . .
A few mules

—Beasts with sad eyes and tired ears—
Carry the earth's
Painful burden,
Their weary steps
Gently tread
The North country's long and lonely roads . . .
The streams have long since dried up
The river beds are full of the traces of wheels,
The earth and the people of the North
Thirstily look for
The flowing springs that nourish life.
Withered trees
And squat houses
Isolated, gloomy
Are scattered below the grey dark sky.
In the sky,
The sun cannot be seen,
Only flocks of geese gathered into droves
Confused geese
Flapping their black wings calling out their restlessness and
    grief
Fleeing from this desolate place
Fleeing to
The green shaded sky of the South . . .

The North is sad
And the endless Yellow River
Churning turbulent waves
Has poured down upon the broad North
Disasters and misfortunes,
And the frost of years
Has carved into the broad North
Poverty and hunger.

And I
—This traveler from the South—
Actually love this gloomy North.
The face-assaulting wind and sand
And bone-penetrating cold
Have never made me curse;
I love this sad land of my country,
The expanse of boundless desert
Arouses my respect
—I see
Our ancestors
Leading flocks of sheep
Blowing on their pipes
Sink into the dusk of this big desert;
We are treading
In the layers of ancient loose earth
Entrusted with our ancestors' bones—
It was this land they pioneered,
Several thousand years ago
They were here
And battled with the nature that struck at them,
To protect their land
They never once bowed to shame,
They have died
And left the land to us—
I love this sad land,
Its huge but lean space
Giving us simplicity of speech
And expansiveness of manner,
I believe that this speech and this manner
Will live on in the big land with strength
Never to be destroyed,
I love this sad land,

This ancient land
—This soil
Has nourished what I love
The most hard-up
The most ancient of races on Earth.

(Translated by Cyril Birch)

EIGHT

POETRY OF REVOLUTION

Confucius, China's first sage, believed in the power of rituals to control the actions of men. He taught that people, when given too much freedom, become headstrong and put self-interest before the good of society. He also knew that to protest against government injustice was necessary, and that revolution was perhaps the ultimate power held by the masses. Confucius said: "One who is by nature daring and is suffering will not long be law-abiding. Indeed, any man, save those that are truly Good, if their sufferings are very great, will be likely to rebel."

In the first half of the twentieth century the Chinese people were suffering. They had fought wars against the imperialist Japanese, rebelled against foreign controls of their seaports, overthrown their corrupt government, attacked their own honored traditions, and died by the hundreds of thousands from these battles and from starvation. Like a body fighting the invasion of a deadly germ, they experimented with one medicine after another, but their immune system was decayed and their condition was weak and unstable. No one could save them but themselves; no nation cared or understood about the lifeline that flowed within them, as a people, for over five thousand years.

On May 4, 1919, the first revolutionary protest of the century took place in Tiananmen Square, where students and intellectuals gathered to protest the ceding of Shandong province to the Japanese. The rebels complained that the Chinese culture and government were not serving the needs of the people; they looked to the West for solutions and found Marxism. While young communists met in dark rooms and hideaways to plan China's future, older statesmen with Western ideas tried to stabilize the inflammation. Dr. Sun Yat-sen, made president of China's First Republic in 1912, and his successor Chiang Kai-shek, who took the reins when Sun died in 1925, fought the Japanese invasion in the north and the communist rebels in the southern mountains. Despite American support of Chiang and the Kuomintang, however, communist forces won the civil war and in 1949 established the People's Republic of China.

Mao Tse-tung, leader of the communist revolution, was a politician and a poet. Like Confucius, Mao believed that a class system orders and controls society and that literature serves the state. In 1942 he declared that literature should be used only as an "instrument of proletarian revolution." All art and culture were "tools for uniting and educating the working people, and weapons for attacking and destroying their class enemies."

Class enemies were easily recognized by their previous high status in Chinese society: the professionals and teachers, rich peasant families and landlords, the intelligentsia and capitalists, as well as counterrevolutionaries. These were stereotyped as bad guys, while industrial workers, farmers and peasants, store clerks and other non-intelligentsia middle class, as well as the revolutionary army, were given hero status.

Government authorities expected artists to subordinate individual visions to the collective interests of the working people, and the state controlled the publication and dissemination of all reading matter. Consequently, much of what was written in China from 1950 to the present has a propagandist quality to it and has been rejected as serious literature.

There are some startling exceptions, however. Even Mao—quite possibly the best Chinese poet of his time, and probably a better poet than a politician, now that the effects of the Cultural Revolution have been examined—wrote poems that are well-crafted and sensitive musings of a people in a campaign so enormous and significant that it astounds the imagination. He had studied the classics and the poetry of earlier times, and he wrote about contemporary events in the classical style, using mythical allusions, traditional symbolism, and the old *shih* and *t'zu* poetic forms. Nothing in his poems bespeaks communist doctrine, regardless of his directive to other creative artists of his time.

Also included among the selections here are folk songs written by the peasants during the 1950s. The government sent writers and teachers into the countryside to encourage the people to write poetry. Contests were held; everyone joined in the creative effort. By the end of the decade national publishers had collected seven hundred volumes of folk songs, with thousands more being collected in the provinces. As in the time of Confucius, these songs reflected the moods and attitudes of the common people. Although they may have been commissioned for political purposes and were undoubtedly censored by editors, as Confucius likely selected carefully among the peasant songs, they do express the simple life in colloquial language. *Songs of the Red Flag* are reminiscent of the ancient *Book of Songs* and provide us with a fresh look at what motivates the Chinese people. Indeed, if Chinese poetry is to continue its magnificent tradition, the heritage of the past must be part of the present, just as political maneuvering of literary arts needs to be viewed as an historic role of Chinese governments.

THE LONG MARCH

MAO TSE-TUNG, 1935

For our Red Army there was no fear in
meeting hardships of the Long March;
those myriad streams to be crossed,
that maze of mountains to be climbed,
simply a part of the work to be done;
crests of the five ranges rising in front
of us as waves over a stormy sea,
yet taken in our passage
as though they were tiny ripples;
the crossing of the rugged Wumeng range
as if it was a lump of clay;
and there was that river of Golden Sands
running by precipices,
lying warm against the sun;
and the long chains of iron
stretching over the gorge of the Tatu River
cold, so cold in our grasp;
then marching through those miles of snow
on Minshan;
and on the faces of all our fighters
was joy.

(Translated by Rewi Alley)

LOUSHAN PASS

MAO TSE-TUNG, 1935

West wind strong
Wild geese honked across the sky; frosty morning moon,
Frosty morning moon.
Broken clatter of horses' hooves,
Bugles' mournful tune.

They said this pass was iron-bound
But striding out we took it in one,
Took it in one.
Green crests like a sea,
Blood the setting sun.

(Translated by Kai-yu Hsu)

BURIAL

HO CHING-CHIH, 1956-58

He didn't come back until very, very late.
The casket carriers, grave diggers had all left,
But he sprawled on the newly dug grave, weeping,
Even those trying to comfort him had gone, long gone,
He still stayed there, his voice hoarse for all that crying.

He didn't come back until very, very late.
The owls in the woods were stirred up by his weeping.
Night had descended over the wilderness,
No stars, no moon,
November, winds howled like wolves.

He didn't come back until very, very late.
Cold gusts of wind whipped him. He struggled up
From the newly dug grave, and walked out of the woods.
Cold wind pushed him, he couldn't see the road.
November, a night in the village, a night of unending sorrow.

He didn't come back until very, very late.
The burial was over, forever underground lay the dead
That had been his brother, his only kin.
Now the debtors were waiting for him at his hut,
To divide up his property, that half-mu of land.

He didn't come back until very, very late.
Passing in front of his hut, he kept going.
Going through one stretch of wilderness, and another.
The November cold wind howled—
He walked on, toward a faraway place, far from his homeland.

(Translated by Kai-yu Hsu)

THE FROG'S CROAK

YEN CHEN, 1959-61

The frog's croak rings outside the village,
Pale moonlight fills the windowpane,
A sleepless captain of the production team
Treads on the moonlight to approach the riverside.

The moon, the frog's croak, and the river tide
Bring back to him a scene ten years old:
A soldier on scout duty, he sneaked across
The Yangtze River to come to the south side.

Pa, pa, pa ... flew the enemy's bullets,
Go, go, go ... he faked a frog's croak;
The enemy, though cunning, was fooled,
Towing his gun he slowly took to the road ...

The frog croaks louder now, the village asleep,
The captain comes to a wheat field—all is calm;
He smiles and bends down to study carefully
That new ear of wheat lying against his palm.

(Translated by Kai-yu Hsu)

CHINESE POETRY

SELECTIONS FROM

SONGS OF THE RED FLAG

ANONYMOUS POEMS BY PEASANTS COLLECTED AND PUBLISHED IN 1961

We are a people who love to sing,
our torrent of songs outstrips the rivers.
First we sang of co-operation,
now we sing of the Great Leap Forward.
Our singing keeps the water and soil on the hills,
our singing makes each acre yield three tons;
our singing fills the hills with flocks and herds,
our singing turns the gullies into goldmines;
and as we sing we'll pass the Yellow River
and make the North resound with Southern songs.

There's no Jade Emperor in the sky,
on earth no Dragon King;
I'm the Jade Emperor myself,
I'm the Dragon King!
I order the Three Mountains and Five Peaks:
    "Make way there,
      here I come!"

In Taihang born, in Taihang bred,
and reared in a cottage of stone on the hills.

I'd never seen a river or wave in my life,
nor known the length of a wooden boat.

But since the commune has been set up
we hill-folk live on the water's edge.

We've cut out rivers across the slopes,
and the clear flowing water is covered with sails.

No more the winding uphill track:
we float up the hillsides poling a boat.

We once herded cattle and sheep on the hills;
today in a river we're casting our nets.

A green and yellow patchwork across the country lies.
The yellow is the ripened corn, the green is growing rice.

Who was it embroidered these colors on the land?
The working people made them, with their two bare
    hands.

We lads in the forging-shop have unbounded strength;
our power-hammer shakes the sky with its sound.
Beneath the hammer a golden dragon writhes
and fills the shop with a glow like sunset clouds.

We lads in the forging-shop find work a joy;
our production graph soars up like a bird on the wing.
Our revolutionary ardor glows like fire
and every day we forge a mountain of steel.

We lads in the forging-shop have an iron will;
we battle beside the hammer day and night.

We throw ourselves into our work to leave Britain
    behind;
we're riding a golden dragon up into the sky.

China has many people and many heroes,
one spade-stroke from each and there's a new river.

China has many people and many stout fellows,
one pick-stroke from each and there's a hill shifted.

China has many people and many artists,
one brush-stroke and there's a new landscape.

China has many people and many poets,
one poem from each and there's more than the stars.

The magpie screams loudly and up his tail goes,
the whole of the co-op is out with their hoes.
My sweetheart and I are leading the line
but he keeps throwing glances at me all the time.

"Dear Brother," I whisper, "stop looking this way,
keep your eyes on your hoeing and don't let them stray;
If you look at me instead of your hoe
you'll let weeds get by and the wheat will not grow."

SPRING THUNDER

HSÜ CH'IH, 1965

Spring thunder explodes, rocking the world.
Up and down the great river, ice has thawed.
The season of frozen mountains is over,
And the era of frozen mountains has come to an end.

Rivers and lakes are swollen with muddy water,
Huge loads of lumber come downriver in peals of songs.
Look at us. Look at how we till the land and build the country
With everyone decked out in light clothes, new gowns.

We open our bright eyes wide, very wide,
To take in our colorful life with infinite joy.
Spring has arrived in a brand new China,
To be followed closely by a spring for all men.

Willows everywhere are swaying in the wind,
Even quiet and solemn wu-t'ung trees have sprouted.
Azaleas bloom, covering the lush mountainsides,
And birds sing their songs to summon travelers.

With a bag on my shoulders and a song on my lips,
I shall go far to the country, to the work sites, and sing
For this world, and look at valleys from hilltops,
And cover me with fallen petals and soak me in rains of spring.

(Translated by Kai-yu Hsu)

HOMESPUN CORRESPONDENT

SHEN YUNG-CH'ANG*, 1971

All quiet late at night,
In the room, under the lamp light,
The homespun correspondent of our team
Seizes his pen in earnest.

Reports, page after page,
Make clear our line of work,
Singing praise of Chairman Mao,
Describing to him our new farm life.

Red hearts turn to the sun;
Broad shoulders bear heavy tasks.
He holds firmly his literary power,
To serve as our responsible spokesman.

Imitate not the ephemeral showings of the night-blooming
 cereus,
But rather learn from the plum blossoms which shun
 crowded springs.
He keeps to his heart the meaning of the "homespun,"
And always writes to serve the revolution.

(Translated by Kai-yu Hsu)

---

*This poet was simply identified as a member of the Shan-yang Commune in a volume of folk verse produced to commemorate the fiftieth anniversary of the founding of the Communist Party in China.

NINE

A NEW POETRY EMERGES

The year 1976 marked a turning point for China's ongoing revolution. Three factions were jousting for control of a shaky regime after the fiasco of the Cultural Revolution*: a Maoist consortium known as The Gang of Four, the moderates under the leadership of Premier Zhou Enlai and Deng Xiaoping, and the army under Lin Biao. In January 1976 Zhou Enlai died and official mourning of his death was forbidden. Tensions grew among the disillusioned youth who were forced to abandon their education after the Cultural Revolution and were shipped to the country by the Gang of Four (seventeen million urban youths were sent to work with the peasants in the early 1970s!). On April 5, 1976, a demonstration in Tiananmen Square followed the repression of a public display of emotion with people, as they had traditionally mourned the death of a beloved leader, presenting

---

*The 1966-69 reign of Red Terror during which Mao attempted to purge the system of "bourgeois attitudes" by pitting armed camps of young people—Red Guards from the good classes and revolting Rebel Guards from the bad classes—against four evils or "Olds": old ideas, culture, customs, and habits. The frenzied teenagers used their newfound power to destroy books, artifacts, and other vestiges of former art and culture and in the process harassed each other in an ideological power struggle and terrorized educators and historians who they perceived as vanguards of the old. One hundred million intellectuals were tortured, imprisoned or killed, according to Chinese figures; possibly 850,000 deaths resulted from beatings and suicides.

poems and wreaths in Zhou's honor. Then, in September 1976, Mao Tse-tung died and the Gang of Four were arrested. Deng Xiaoping was reinstated as Premier and the young people were allowed to return to the cities. The new priority was to focus on the economy and to strengthen China's resources in the Four Modernizations: agriculture, industry, science and technology, and defense.

In 1979 some 500,000 intellectuals were "rehabilitated" and in 1982 intellectuals were added to the official list of people building China, along with soldiers, peasants, and workers. This new generation, men and women in their forties who had survived the horrors of the middle decades but had lost opportunities to further their education and find good jobs, are now questioning the political system rather than the leaders. Historians refer to this alienated group as the Mao generation, manipulated by their leaders in political power struggles. From this generation has emerged the democratic movement that led to the June 4, 1989, protest in Tiananmen Square.

A New Realism appeared in Chinese literature—a short "thaw" from 1977 to 1981 gave us a look at the current literature, in which writers were allowed to criticize the Cultural Revolution and the radical policies of the Gang of Four. Deng's position was that the government should lead, not control, the arts, but he asked artists (many of whom had never used their talents except to further the revolution) to consider the social impact of their work. A 1983 campaign, however, was launched to rid Chinese literature of three evils: humanism, existentialism, and modernism.

Writers struggle with the concept of *human* nature vs *class* nature, the theoretical basis for the difference between socialism and democracy. Can their characters from *good* classes exhibit bad qualities and characters from *bad* classes appear good? According to Annie Dillard, the American author who traveled with a group of literary emissaries to China and helped host a returning visit from Chinese writers in 1982, this question may be presumptuous. She writes:

> China is the only one of the world's great early civilizations that still exists—this, in spite of its crippling geography, its beautiful, mostly barren and famishing land. The Chinese people have done what the Babylonians, the Greeks, the Persians, and the Romans were unable to do. By their own efforts, they have kept their country going; they have kept it whole.*

Poetry has always been a vehicle of protest in China, even though writers do not have the freedom of speech of which we Americans are so staunchly protective. They want it all: cultural integrity, economic and political independence, a sense of the past and a promise of the future, and the knowledge that all the bloodshed and pain was worthwhile. Shu Ting's poem "Perhaps" asks these questions with the sensitivity of a woman revolutionary in conflict.

Many Chinese left mainland China during the revolution and found refuge in Taiwan, the United States, and other countries. Although much of their poetry is very Western in style and subject, it contains a poignant rebellion of its own and is represented here by the poetry of Yu Kwang-chung, Lo Fu, and Huang Guobin.

The poetry of the new Mao generation is fueled with the energy of a people moving forward and fused with a

---

*From *Encounters With Chinese Writers*, by Annie Dillard (Middleton, Conn: Wesleyan University Press, 1984), p. 32.

tentative alliance with a most formidable past. The young poets are forging their own expressions, having neither the new influence of Western literature to seduce them nor the old ties with classical poetry to inhibit them.

Where to go next? The world watches as China grapples with its 1200 million people and their needs. And we listen to the expressions of the people who know the power of a line of poetry.

WHEN I AM DEAD

YU KWANG-CHUNG, 1966

When I am dead, lay me down between the Yangtze
And the Yellow River and pillow my head
On China, white hair against black soil,
Most beautiful, O most maternal of lands,
And I will sleep my soundest taking
The whole mainland for my cradle, lulled
By the mother-hum that rises on both sides
From the great rivers, two long, long songs
That on and on flow forever to the East.
This the world's most indulgent roomiest bed
Where, content, a heart pauses to rest
And recalls how, of a Michigan winter night,
A youth from China used to keep
Intense watch towards the East, trying
To pierce his look through darkness for the dawn
Of China. So with hungry eyes he devoured
The map, eyes for seventeen years starved
For a glimpse of home, and, like a new weaned child,
He drank with one wild gulp rivers and lakes
From the mouth of the Yangtze all the way up
To Poyang and Tungting and to Koko Nor.

(Translated by the poet)

SONG OF THE CRICKET

LO FU

SOMEONE ONCE SAID, "OVERSEAS, I HEARD A CRICKET SING, AND THOUGHT IT WAS THE ONE I HEARD WHEN I WAS IN THE COUNTRYSIDE OF SZECHUAN."

Carrying from the courtyard
To the corner of the wall:
Jit, Jut . . . jit, jut.
Out of the stone crevice
Suddenly jumping
To a pillow under the white hairs,
Jut, jut.
Pushed from yesterday's drifting
To this day's corner of the world,
The cricket sings
But hides its head, its legs, wings.
I grope everywhere,
High in the sky, deep in the earth.
Still it is invisible.
I even tear open my breast,
But fail to find that vibrator.
The evening rain just then stopped.
The moon outside the window
Delivers the axe sound of a woodcutter.
The stars are seething.
And the cricket's song bubbling
Like a stream.
My childhood drifts from upstream,
But tonight I am not in Ch'en-tu,
And my snores do not mean nostalgia.

Unceasing is the cricket song in my ears,
A thousand-threaded tune;
I have forgotten the year, the month, the evening,
Which city or town,
In which bus depot I have heard this song.
Jut, jut . . . jit, jut.
Tonight, however, more shocking.
The cricket's cry
Meanders like River Chai-ling by my pillow.
Deep in night
With no boat to hire;
I can only swim, follow the tides
Where the waves of the Three Gorges are sky-high
And monkeys shriek by the river bank,
And fish,
Only hot spicy bean fish lie in a green porcelain platter.
Jut, jut.
Which cricket is really singing?
The Cantonese one sings the loneliest,
The Szechuan the saddest,
And the Peking cricket, the noisiest.
But the Hunan cricket sings
With the taste of spicy heat.
Yet what finally woke me
Was the one in the lane at San-chang Li,
The softest, the dearest
Singing of all.

(Translated by Dominic Cheung)

MY POEM

HUANG GUOBIN, 1978

My poem is a bridge, silent, lonely;
For long, long years, it bears my tribesmen, a simple people,
Helps them cross rivers, climb hills; in the morning and evening
It reaches out to the village in smoke, in the light of dawn.

My poem is a well, old, alone;
Through the ages it listens to the swallows as they come and go,
Watches the folk as they wash and cook by the well,
Listens to footsteps as they move away, as they draw near.

My poem is a song, distant, lasting,
Hidden in the countless gorges, in the breathing of the sea;
When crowds disperse, cries and clamour die down,
It rises lightly, like the sea-gull in the wind.

My poem is a star, remote, steadfast,
Resisting the heartless cold in the void beyond light years.
Deep in the night, when the air is no more polluted by the neon lights,
Its brilliance will linger on, in the eyes that look up to the sky.

(Translated by Mok Wing-yin and the poet)

LONGING

SHU TING, 1980

A hanging scroll in a swirl of colors, lacking line
An algebraic formula, simple but unsolvable
A one-stringed lute, strumming a rosary of raindrops from
    the eaves
A pair of oars that never reach the opposite shore

Silently waiting, like a swelling bud
Distantly gazing, like the setting sun
Somewhere, perhaps, a vast ocean lurks
But only two tears trickle out

O in the vistas of the heart
In the depths of the soul

(Translated by Helen F. Siu and Zelda Stern)

PERHAPS

SHU TING, 1980

Perhaps our cares
   will never have readers
Perhaps the journey that was wrong from the start
   will be wrong at the end
Perhaps every single lamp we have lit
   will be blown out by the gale
Perhaps when we have burned out our lives to lighten the
   darkness
   there will be no warming fire at our sides.

Perhaps when all the tears have flowed
   the soil will be richer
Perhaps when we sing of the sun
   the sun will sing of us
Perhaps as the weight on our shoulders grows heavier
   our faith will be more lofty
Perhaps we should shout about suffering as a whole
   but keep silent over personal grief.

Perhaps
Because of an irresistible call
We have no other choice.

(Translated by W. J. F. Jenner)

TEMPTATION

QIU XIAOLONG, 1981

Soft are the arms
That press me to your bosom:
"Stay—listen—here is your still haven,
Embrace me, and no harm can come to us."

Sweet are the lips
That pout to mine:
"Stay—look—a bud that blossoms for you,
Kiss me, and we'll get drunk on joy."

But when I lift my head, I hear
The speedboat churn the waves across the boundless ocean,
    I see
The white trail left by the jet that roars across the sky, and
    I feel
That there are many things beyond my knowing, that I
    would know.

(Translated by Bonnie S. McDougall and the poet)

THE OLD TEMPLE

BEI DAO, 1983?

The fading chimes
form cobwebs, spreading a series of annual rings
among the splintered columns
without a memory, a stone
spreads an echo through the misty valley
a stone, without memory
when a small path wound a way here
the dragons and strange birds flew off
carrying away the mute bells under the eaves
once a year weeds
grow, indifferently
not caring whether the master they submit to
is a monk's cloth shoe, or wind
the stele is chipped, the writing on its surface worn away
as if only in a general conflagration
could it be deciphered, yet perhaps
with a glance from the living
the tortoise might come back to life in the earth
and crawl over the threshold, bearing its heavy secret

(Translated by Bonnie S. McDougall)

CHINESE POETRY

—FOR THE VICTIMS OF JUNE FOURTH

REQUIEM

BEI DAO, 1989

Not the living but the dead
under the doomsday-purple sky
go in groups
suffering guides forward suffering
at the end of hatred is hatred
the spring has run dry, the conflagration stretches
    unbroken
the road back is even further away

Not gods but the children
amid the clashing of helmets
say their prayers
mothers breed light
darkness breeds mothers
the stone rolls, the clock runs backwards
the eclipse of the sun has already appeared

Not your bodies but your souls
shall share a common birthday every year
you are all the same age
love has founded for the dead
an ever-lasting alliance
you embrace each other closely
in the massive register of deaths

*(Translated by Bonnie S. McDougall
and Chen Maiping)*

MOTHER, I'M HUNGRY

YU KWANG-CHUNG, 1989

Mother, I'm hungry,
But I cannot swallow.
Such a bitter taste
Chokes my throat all day long:
How can I swallow?

Mother, I'm tired,
But I cannot sleep.
Such a heavy feeling
Weighs on my chest all night long:
How can I sleep?

Mother, I'm dead,
But I'm not resigned.
Such a tortured country
Brands my soul forever;
How can I give up?

Mother, I'm gone.
On Tomb-Sweeping Day*
Come back to recall my soul
In democratic years
In Tiananmen Square.

(Translated by the poet)

---

*Chinese festival in spring when family members gather to attend the tomb of the deceased and offer sacrifice.

EPIGRAPH

GU GHENG, 1980

In the sea of life,
Hold firm the rudder
Don't, because of a favorable wind,
Be drawn into a whirlpool
For the time being, let running aground
Be a precious little rest.
Calmly watch the complacent sails
Ride with the waves.

*(Translated by Helen F. Siu
and Zelda Stern)*

ACKNOWLEDGMENTS

Grateful acknowledgment is made to the following for permission to reprint previously published material:

SIR HAROLD ACTON AND ARTELLUS LIMITED: "Midnight" by Hsauu Chih-mo translated by Sir Harold Acton from *Modern Chinese Poetry*. Copyright © Harold Acton.

CHINESE LITERATURE PRESS: "The Roebuck" and "Boat of Cypress Wood" from *Selections from the Book of Songs* published by Chinese Literature Press in 1983.

COLUMBIA UNIVERSITY PRESS: "The Wind" by Sung Yu, "Lovely the Young Peach Tree," "The Lord Among the Clouds" by Chu Yuan, "Li Sao" by Ch'u Yuan from *Early Chinese Literature*, translated by Burton Watson. "Blaming Sons" by Tao Yuan-ming from *The Columbia Book of Chinese Poetry*, translated by Burton Watson. "Nineteen Poems of the Han," "Matching a Poem by Secretary Kuo" by Tao Yuan-ming, "Restless Night" by Tu Fu, "A Traveler at Night Writes His Thoughts" by Tu Fu, "The Dappled Horse" by Mei Yao-ch'en, "Farm Families" by Lu Yu from *Chinese Lyricism* translated by Burton Watson. "To the Tune, Nan-hsiang-tzu" by Shen Chou, "A Painting of the Butterfly Dream by the Master Artist Li Tsai" by Chu Yun-ming, "A Lady Picking Flowers" by Shen Chou, "Finding Serenity" by Yuan Mei, "New Year's Eve" by Liu E from *The Columbia Book of Later Chinese Poetry* translated by Jonathan Chaves. "Song of the Cricket" by Lo Fu from *The Ilse of Noises: Modern Chinese Poetry from Taiwan* edited by Dominic Cheung. Reprinted by permission of Columbia University Press.

DOUBLEDAY: "Old Dream" by Hu Shih, "Rebirth of Spring" by Hsu Chih-mo, "Deliverance" by Ping Hsin, "Impressions of Shanghai" by Kuo Mo-jo, "Sonnet XVI" by Feng Chih from *Twentieth Century Chinese Poetry* by Kai-yu Hsu. Copyright © 1963 by Kai-yu Hsu. Reprinted by permission of Doubleday, a division of Bantam Doubleday Dell Publishing Group, Inc. "At Yellow Crane Tower, Seeing Off Meng Hau-ran on His Way to Jang-jou" by Li Bai and "Jade Stairs Resentment" by Li Bai from *The Heart of Chinese Poetry* translated by Greg Whincup. Copyright © 1987 by Greg Whincup. Reprinted by permission of Doubleday, a division of Bantam Doubleday Dell Publishing Group, Inc. and John Farquharson Ltd.

GROVE PRESS, INC.: "Tall Stands that Pear Tree," "Rabbit Goes Soft-foot," "King Wen's Park Divine," and "On the Mountain" from *Anthology of Chinese Literature*, Volume I, edited by Cyril Birch. Copyright © 1965 by Grove Press, Inc. "The North" from *Anthology of Chinese Literature*, Volume II, edited by Cyril Birch. Copyright © 1972 by Grove Press, Inc. Reprinted by permission of Grove Press, Inc.

HILL AND WANG: "The Old Temple" by Bei Dao from *Seeds of Fire* edited by Geremie Barmé and John Binford. Copyright © 1988 by Geremie Barmé and John Minford. Reprinted by permission of Hill and Wang, a division of Farrar, Straus and Giroux, Inc.

HOUGHTON MIFFLIN COMPANY: "Drinking Alone in the Moonlight" from *The Complete Poetical Works of Amy Lowell* by Amy Lowell. Copyright © 1955 by Houghton Mifflin Co. Copyright ©1953 by Houghton Mifflin Co., Brinton P. Roberts, and G. D'Andelot Belin, Esquire. Reprinted by permission of Houghton Mifflin Co.

INDIANA UNIVERSITY PRESS: "In a Boat, Getting Up at Night" by Su Shih, "For Contemporary Artist Pien Wei-ch'i" by Cheng Hsieh, "Tune: Song of the Lunar Palace" by Kuan Yun-shih, "Bitter Cold" by Po Chu-i from *Sunflower Splendor* by Wu-chi Liu and Irving Y. Lo. "At LouShan Pass" by Mao, "Burial" by Ho Ching-Chih, "The Frog's Croak" by Yen Chen, "Spring Thunder" by Hsu Ch'ih, "Homespun Correspondent" by Shen Yung-ch'ang from *Literature of The People's Republic of China* edited by Kai-yu Hsu and Ting Wang. "Perhaps" by Shu Ting and "Temptation" by Qiu Xiaolong from *Stubborn Weeds* edited by Perry Link.

ALFRED A. KNOPF, INC.: "To Li Po at the Sky's End" from *The Jade Mountain: A Chinese Anthology* by Witter Bynner. Copyright 1929 and renewed 1957 by Alfred A. Knopf, Inc. Reprinted by permission of Alfred A. Knopf, Inc. "The Poem on the Wall" by Po Chu-i and "Woman" by Fu Hsuan from *Translations from the Chinese* by Arthur Waley. Copyright 1919 and renewed 1947 by Arthor Waley. Reprinted by permission of Alfred A. Knopf, Inc. and Unwin Hyman of HarperCollins Publishers Limited.

NEW DIRECTIONS PUBLISHING CORPORATION: "Jade Flower Palace" by Tu Fu from *One Hundred Poems from the Chinese* translated by Kenneth Rexroth. Copyright © 1971 by Kenneth Rexroth. "On a Visit to Chung Chen Taoist Temple . . ." by Yu Hsuan-chi, "Willow Eyebrows" by Chao Luan-Luan, "To the Tune a Hilly Garden" by Li Ching-chao, "Spring Joy" by Chu Shu-chen, "To the Tune Red Embroidered Shoes" by Huang O, "Seeking a Mooring" by Wang Wei from *Women Poets of China* by Kenneth Rexroth. Copyright © 1972 by Kenneth Rexroth and Ling Chung. Reprinted by permission of New Directions Publishing Corporation.

NORTH POINT PRESS: Eleven poems by Han-shan from *Riprap and Cold Mountain Poems* translated by Gary Snyder. Copyright © 1965 by Gary Snyder. Published by North Point Press and reprinted by permission.

HAROLD OBER ASSOCIATES INC.: "Requiem" by Bei Dao from *New Directions 54*, to be included in *Old Snow*, New Directions. Copyright © 1990 by New Directions Pub. Corp. Reprinted by permission of Harold Ober Associates Inc.

OXFORD UNIVERSITY PRESS, INC.: "Longing" by Shu Ting and "Epigraph" by Gu Cheng from *Mao's Harvest: Voices from China's New Generation* by Helen F. Siu and Zelda Stern. Copyright © 1983 by Helen F. Siu and Zelda Stern. Reprinted by permission of Oxford University Press, Inc.

RESEARCH CENTRE FOR TRANSLATION: "My Poem" by Huang Guobin reprinted from Renditions, Nos. 19 & 20 (Spring & Autumn, 1983), published by The Research Centre for Translation, The Chinese University of Hong Kong.

CHARLES E. TUTTLE CO., INC.: "Composed on a Spring Day on the Farm" from *Poems by Wang Wei*, translated by Chang Yin-nan and Lewis C. Walmsley. Reprinted by permission of Charles E. Tuttle Co., Inc. of Tokyo, Japan.